HOW TO CATCH A GROOM

HOW TO CATCH A GROOM

HOLLY JACOBS

Ilex Books 2019
ISBN-13: 978-1-948311-02-1

Originally published
Harlequin Books
Copyright © 2002 by Holly Fuhrmann.

REVIEWS

"Funny and charming, Holly Jacobs's HOW TO CATCH A GROOM (4) beautifully captures the fear and elation of falling in love. Her heroine is easy to relate to, and her slightly nerdy hero is adorable."
~ RT Bookclub

"Holly Jacobs gives us a non-stereotypical hero. Readers can't help but fall for in her slightly nerdy scientist Seth Rutherford, whose logical, practical brain nearly leads him down the aisle with the wrong woman in HOW TO CATCH A GROOM."
~ RT WISH Award
(Women in Search of Heroes)

"Logic and emotion both have a place in life... and love. Ms. Jacobs' story proves that, and it is a delightful one. She is a wonderfully talented author who is making her mark in romance. Why not try a few others of her books as well?"
~ Loves Romance—4.5

"She makes you laugh and cry..."
~ Writers Unlimited

"Outrageous and witty, HOW TO CATCH A GROOM is a delightful story of two people brought together in the most unexpected way. A great read, lots of fun, and wonderfully written, I highly recommend it!"

~ Escape to Romance Reviewer—4.5

"In the end our hero and heroine get together, but Holly Jacob's makes them earn every sentence and scene to get there. Yes, this story made me laugh and it held my interest as all of Holly's books do. How to Catch a Groom proved to be a story of love and pure comical entertainment."

~ Women on Writing

"What a fun book! Escape the ordinary and Catch this pair of funny and charming love stories!"

~ All About Romance

PROLOGUE

"Size matters. Size always matters." Mrs. O'Malley, the mother of the bride-to-be, gave a little *humph* for emphasis. "And my daughter won't put up with something inferior."

"Ma'am, I've seen it myself, and it's big enough. Plenty big," Desi Smith soothed.

Soothing was part of her job as the wedding coordinator, but she feared it would take a double-strength shot of a strong sedative to truly soothe this woman.

"Seth, there you are," Mrs. O'Malley cried, looking past Desi to the blond groom-to-be. "Help me out here, will you?"

"Sure, if I can, ma'am."

"Mom. I've told you, call me Mom. Not that I look old enough to be your mother," she hastily added, patting her perfectly coifed brunette hair. "Now, I want you to tell this girl that size does matter. It matters a lot. Mary Kathryn needs it big. If it's too small she'll be disappointed. And I don't want her disappointed by something that is inferior."

Seth Rutherford's eyes widened and he cleared his throat before he replied slowly, "Uh . . . just what are we talking about here?"

Desi tried not to smile as she realized how their conversation might be misconstrued. "We're talking about the wedding cake. Mrs. O'Malley is afraid it's not big enough for all the guests. I've been reassuring her that it is."

"Oh, *the cake*." Seth looked relieved.

"Well, I'm going to go find Mary Kathryn. I think you're both wrong and she'll be disappointed tomorrow." Mrs. O'Malley made her way to the opposite end of The Bayside's banquet room. Mrs. O'Malley had insisted on only the very best for her daughter's rehearsal dinner, and Bayside was the best Erie, Pennsylvania had to offer.

Desi was sure she hadn't heard the end of the cake issue, but was grateful for the reprieve.

"Do I know you?" Seth asked unexpectedly.

"Pardon?" Desi asked.

"I said, do I know you? You look familiar, but I haven't been able to place where I might know you from."

Desi smiled. "I was wondering if you'd remember. We went to high school together. I was in the Gifted Program, too, though I was a few years behind you."

What she didn't add was that she'd spent a great portion of her sophomore year fantasizing about the sandy-haired senior. Or that she'd cut his picture from the newspaper when he'd won the science fair and hung it by her vanity mirror.

Heck, she'd even doodled his name and hers together.

He shook his head. "I'm sorry, I don't remember you."

"I've changed a lot. Back then I had braces, was painfully skinny, and had horribly frizzy hair."

Thankfully, as she'd let her hair grow out, the fizziness had abated, she'd foregone glasses in favor of contacts, and of course, what was skinny in high school was slender and in vogue as an adult. She certainly wasn't gorgeous, but she felt she'd improved with age.

Seth studied her a moment, and finally said, "Sorry. Still drawing a blank."

"The Science Fair? My table was next to yours and—"

"That was you? That's why you look familiar. I was so nervous. I spent the better part of three months working on that project and when I discovered the missing transistor, I figured I'd lost the competition for sure. But then you handed me one and said it was a spare," he stared at her for moment, and then added slowly. "Only it wasn't spare at all, was it? I didn't find out until later you took it off your own project."

"The science fair didn't mean that much to me." Desi shrugged. "It was more for my Mom and Dad. Anyway, it was no biggie."

"It was very big to me. That scholarship helped me get through college. I've always wished I could repay you."

"I didn't do it because I wanted your gratitude."

"Why did you do it?" he asked.

Desi wasn't about to answer that particular question. After all, he hadn't known about her crush in high school, so why give it away now?

She just smiled and said, "I really should get back and check on things in the kitchen."

Before she could turn and make her retreat, Seth said, "I never would have known you, even though you looked familiar. You don't look anything like you did then."

Desi smiled. "And for that I'm eternally grateful. High school definitely ranks as my awkward phase."

"Awkward?" He laughed. "I never quite outgrew that phase. I'm still awkward. I tripped at the rehearsal when I walked Mary Kathryn down the aisle and I've already spilled wine and dinner hasn't even started. I can't wait until it's over. I hate social functions."

"That's why I'm here. To make this as easy on you as possible."

1

"If you can simply keep me from making a fool of myself, I'll be eternally grateful."

"I'll do my best."

He smiled.

Desi remembered that smile from her school days. It hadn't changed at all. And for some reason, she was glad for that.

Mary Kathryn, the bride-to-be, gave a little wave from across the room, and Desi pulled herself back to the present. "I think your bride wants you."

He turned and waved back to Mary Kathryn. "See you tomorrow," he called over his shoulder.

Desi watched as her first official crush walked across the room to his bride-to-be and best man. He remembered the transistor she'd given him after all these years.

Her small gesture had helped him get a scholarship. She'd rescued him. The thought warmed her.

Once upon a time, she'd dreamed about being at Seth's wedding—only then she'd been the bride, not the wedding planner. Desi smiled at the memory. She'd long since outgrown childhood dreams. She had a job to do, and couldn't wait until the wedding tomorrow. She had a feeling it was going to be something to remember.

CHAPTER ONE

"She's hot-to-trot."

Desi silently agreed with Phil's assessment. The *she* in question was going to trot right out of her own wedding. The bride was about to bolt before the I-do's were said.

"Want me to tackle her?" he asked.

Desi turned and couldn't help form a small smile at the hopeful look on the photographer-working-as-her-assistant's face. "I don't think that will work."

There wasn't a thing either of them could do. They'd watched as the ceremony began, and Desi had felt nervous right from the beginning. The bride-to-be wasn't behaving right. Nervous was one thing, terrified was another. She watched helplessly as the bride ran right down the long aisle and out the door.

"Now what?" Phil muttered.

Desi wished she knew. She'd been coordinating weddings for the last five years and had never had a run-away bride before. She wasn't quite sure what the protocol was for something like that.

"I guess we thank everyone for coming?" she halfway asked. She remembered her promise to Seth the night before and added, "And we try to keep the groom from looking foolish."

"There's no *we* about it, babe. I just snap the pictures and follow orders, you're the one in charge."

She raked her fingers through her long hair, more out of frustration than to push it out of her face.

Desi discreetly fought through the crowd pressed around the groom. She'd made a promise to Seth and she was bound and determined to keep it. "Seth, do you want me to just send everyone home?"

"The reception's paid for, right?" Shannon, the maid-of-honor, sister-of-the-bride, asked.

"Everything's paid for and ready."

"Everything's ready but the bride, I guess," Seth said.

"No use wasting it, Seth," the almost-sister-in-law said.

"I don't want—"

"Listen, let's just show everyone how much class you've got," Shannon pressed.

"Seth?" Desi asked.

She didn't want him to be pushed into anything he didn't want to do. His back was ramrod straight and tension radiated from his very stance. His expression didn't give away any of his feelings, but his eyes... there she could see his pain and confusion in those deep blue eyes and wanted nothing more than to make both disappear.

He shrugged. "Let's party."

Seth Rutherford felt foolish.

He'd been comforted by just about everyone at the reception, and it hadn't helped him feel better, it had simply made him more uncomfortable. His mother was so upset that his father had taken her home about fifteen minutes ago.

Seth didn't know how to deal with such free-flowing feelings. His parents wore their emotions like garments, changing them at the slightest provocation. He'd never known how to be like that and, truth be told, had never really wanted to. Such wild emotional ups and downs made him nervous. He was the type to think things through, though obviously he hadn't thought enough about his relationship with Mary Kathryn.

He took a long swig of beer and grimaced. He didn't really like the taste, but he was getting used to it tonight.

He glanced at his watch. He'd lasted two hours at his almost-reception. It was one hour and fifty-nine minutes too long in his opinion.

He'd done his bit, played the good sport, but he was ready to go. He snuck quietly from the hall into the parking lot.

Half of Erie seemed to have come to the reception. Who knew he and Mary Kathryn knew so many people? They lived quiet lives. They weren't exactly people people.

People people. The term made him want to laugh, but he wasn't sure why. Maybe he'd had a few beers too many?

What was he thinking about?

Oh, Mary Kathryn and how he'd always felt at home with her. Since she'd first joined the faculty at the University, he'd felt a connection. He'd invited her to work on his research project and when she'd said yes, that connection had grown. Balancing his teaching schedule and research interests didn't leave much time for a social life, even if he'd wanted one. But Seth had always been more comfortable with books and microscopes than with people.

Until Mary Kathryn.

She had a brilliant mind, and yes, he was comfortable with her. It's one of the reasons he'd decided to marry her—they were a good fit. Common interests, common goals. They should be the perfect couple.

But she was gone.

He took a healthy swig of his beer. He wasn't a *drinking* man, but tonight he was going to make an exception. Although he'd been drinking for the last two hours, it wasn't enough to numb his feelings, whatever they were.

How did he feel about Mary Kathryn? That was the question that had plagued him since she'd left. He loved her… of course he'd loved her. He'd asked her to marry him, hadn't he?

Or had he?

It was just sort of an assumption that they'd marry. Come to think of it, he couldn't even remember picking out a day. However he couldn't seem to focus on much right now. He felt sort of thick and fuzzy, but not quite numb.

Well, thick and fuzzy was preferable to sharp and hurting. With two spare cans of beer tucked in his tux's pockets, he started looking around the parking lot for his car. If he were lucky no one would notice he was gone until he was gone.

The thought seemed sort of convoluted, but Seth didn't let it bother him. He was beyond being bothered tonight.

He was going to just take his thick and fuzzy self home and forget his almost-wedding. He was going to forget women, period.

He didn't need a woman messing up his well-ordered life.

"Seth, can I help you?"

He jumped at the sound of a voice and turned. Ah, the wedding coordinator. Little Desi Smith. Only she wasn't little any more. Oh, she wasn't tall, but she was definitely all grown up.

"Seth? Let me help," she said.

He realized he hadn't responded. "If I hadn't sworn off women, I might consider letting you help me, but as it is, I think I'm better off on my own."

Even if he was forgetting about women, he could still admire their assets and the tiny brunette standing in front of him had some worth admiring.

After last night, he'd gone and pulled out his yearbook and found her. Desdemona Smith. If she hadn't told him, he would have never connected her with his *transistor* girl of so many years ago.

Gone was the awkward looking teenager from the picture. The adult version was a real looker. Short, but well packaged. She had miles of dark brown hair. He wondered what it would feel like to run his fingers through it. It looked silky.

He was more than a little loaded if he was thinking about Desi Smith's hair. Seth was an intellectual. He didn't notice things like that. That he was noticing things about this practical stranger just went to prove he had to get out of here.

"Do you know where my car is?"

"Seth, you can't drive," she said.

"Sure I can. Oh, that was the only test I ever flunked, but I passed it the second time around and have been driving all these years without even one accident. Not even a ticket."

She shook her head and that long, brown, silky hair rippled against her shoulders. He started to reach out for it, but wasn't quite drunk enough to do it. Instead he stuffed his hand in his pocket, feeling a spare beer, cold and moist within it.

"That's not what I meant," she said. "I'm afraid you've had too much to drink to be driving tonight."

"Oh, no, I haven't had nearly enough. I'm thick and fuzzy, but not quite numb." No, if he'd had enough, he'd have forgotten about his almost-wedding and he'd be running his fingers through this woman's hair.

"Well, you've had too much to drive."

"I have to leave. I'm afraid if I don't, I'll make a bigger fool of myself."

"Well, I think you've handled yourself admirably. Everyone does. But why don't you let me drive you," she said softly.

"I—"

"You might as well say yes because there's no way I'm letting you get behind the wheel of a car."

"You're a bossy lady." Seth didn't like bossy ladies. He liked quiet women. Partners. Not someone who thought she had to run the show.

"My friend says I only hired him so he has to listen to me. He says I'm a control freak. A bossy, control freak."

"Mary Kathryn was never bossy."

"I'm not Mary Kathryn," Desi reminded him as she started directing him toward her car.

"I'm glad you're not. She left me. You'd think that was why I was drinking, but the sad truth of it is, she was right."

"Seth, I'm so sorry—"

"Don't be. I owe you for getting me out of here."

Desi led him to a small VW Beetle that had *Engaging Styles* painted across the front hood.

"Just climb in." She unlocked the passenger door.

Seth peeked in and backed out. "Oh, no. I take back owing you. That car's a mess. It's a health hazard. I'm not going to get in there. I'll catch some disease or something."

"It's not that bad," Desi said.

"Well, I'm not going to fit anyway. I'm bigger than a tiny little elf like you and there's no way I'm going to fit in there."

He sat on the seat and tried to squeeze his legs in. He couldn't seem to get them to bend enough to fit, so he didn't make much progress.

"The physical universe is very specific about its laws," he continued, "and guys as big as me don't fit in spaces this small. It's a matter of mass. I could make an equation for you. Hm, would you say I was a cube, or a sphere? If I'm a sphere you just take a cube of my radius and times it by pi and then by four thirds and ..."

Seth realized that Desi didn't seem interested in the equation. As a matter of fact, she didn't say a word as she leaned over and bent his knees for him and crammed his legs into the car.

Seth was surprised he fit.

"If I'd done that equation I would have figured out I could fit with the proper force. See, I remembered mass, but forgot what force can do. I don't normally forget things. So maybe the alcohol is working after all and I'll forget this day."

He paused a moment. "Nope, I remember."

"You are definitely more of a cube than a sphere. But either way, buckle up."

He did what he was told, but muttered the entire time as the woman shut the door and got in the driver's seat. He was right, she was bossy.

That he was right lightened his mood. He'd been wrong about Mary Kathryn, but he was right about this bossy woman.

"Where to?"

"27 Winston Lane," he said as he tossed the empty beer can into the back.

"Hey, you don't have to make a mess."

"Of course I do. This car expects it. I'm surprised you could get a passenger in here, what with all the junk you haul around."

"It's not junk. It's stuff I might need. I do a lot of my work out of this car and I like to be prepared."

"Like a Girl Scout." She didn't look like any scout he'd ever seen. He popped the top of another can as he chuckled.

"It's not that funny," she said. "And why don't you lay off the beer?"

"It *is* funny and I don't want to." So there. He'd told her.

They were both silent as the Bug drove them through downtown Erie and toward his street on the west side of town.

Bug.

It was an appropriate term for this vehicle. The car was little and dirty, just like a bug. Okay, not dirty, but cluttered.

If bugs had compartments, he bet they'd be as cluttered as this car was. Seth would never have cluttered compartments. He liked things neat and orderly. That's why marrying Mary Kathryn had made perfect sense. But now he wasn't marrying her, he discovered that made even more sense, which boggled his mind. After all, two diametrically opposite courses of action shouldn't both make sense.

"Which one?" Desi asked as they made their way up the quiet side street.

"The white one," Seth said.

He'd made it. He was home. All he wanted to do was crawl in his house and forget this day had ever happened. He wasn't going to try to make sense out of what made sense and what didn't. See, he couldn't even make a coherent thought, so how did he expect to make sense?

He was going to just forget about women and marriage and get on with his life. It was summer vacation and he didn't have any classes to teach until next fall. He did have his cat and his research. Who needed anything more than that?

Anxious to start forgetting, he tried to open the Bug's door, but couldn't seem to find the handle, and when he did, the door still wouldn't open.

"Did you lock me in?" he asked. "It would be just like a bossy woman to lock a man in her car. Bossy women like to be in control and if a man can't get out of her car, then she's totally in control. I bet you think I owe you for driving me home."

Even in his alcohol-muddled mind he realized that he probably did.

"It's all part of the job."

"Driving the jilted groom home? I don't think so. I guess I do owe you."

Desi got out of the car without saying a word. She walked around the front end and opened the passenger door. "There you go."

"Oh. Thanks." He tried to get out, but couldn't seem to budge from the seat. "See, I told you your car was too small. I'm stuck. Now you're going to have to call 911, and they'll have to pry me out of here. Oh, that's just great. Just one more humiliation to add to today. Being pried from a flower-child, sixties-flashback, rainbow-painted, messy, little Bug. Well, I can take it. I'm a man."

He popped the top of his last beer. If he was going to be humiliated again, he wanted to be prepared this time.

Desi didn't say a word, she just leaned into the car.

"What are you doing?" he yelled. She was in the way and he couldn't get his can of beer to his lips. And he needed that beer. He wasn't numb enough yet.

And even worse, her *assets* brushed against him. They weren't huge, but they weren't too small. They were big enough for him to have noticed them before and big enough to stick out and graze him as she leaned over him.

The thought *more than a handful's a waste* seemed stuck dead-center in his brain, just like Desi's assets seemed stuck in front of him.

"I don't remember you having breasts in high school. Especially not perky little ones. Where did they come from?"

"You're a scientist, figure it out," Desi said, annoyance tinging her voice.

She moved out of the car and waited. Seth stumbled to his feet and then right into her. She barely caught him but she did indeed catch him.

"You're stronger than you look." He paused, concentrating on drinking his beer while moving his feet toward the house. Maybe he was drunker than he thought?

He might be, but Seth wasn't so drunk that he couldn't pick up on Desi's exasperation. But he was drunk enough to think annoying her was sort of fun.

Desi concentrated on keeping Seth upright as she practically pulled him up the front stairs. He was a big guy. Okay, five foot eight wasn't huge, but it was big to her five feet and three inches.

"I don't need help," Seth mumbled.

"I know."

He paused and said, "Maybe I do a little. Maybe you could help by telling me why Mary Kathryn left me? We were perfect together."

Desi gritted her teeth as they attempted each of the five stairs that led to Seth's porch. She had felt sorry for the deserted groom until she had to halfway carry the drunken ox. He was heavy.

"Sometimes perfection is highly overrated," she said, still struggling with the weight of him.

"But that's not logical. One should always stribe... strite... *try* for perfection." It took him two tries to move to the final step.

"Whoever said love is logical?" Desi asked. She might not be a scientist, but she knew for a fact that love and logic were totally opposite conditions.

"Love? Who said anything about love?"

Desi tried to catch her breath as she practically heaved him onto the porch. "You didn't love Mary Kathryn?"

"Well, certainly I do…did, but not in some romanticized context. We were friends, colleagues, and perfectly suited. Marriage was the next logical step."

Rather than feeling triumphant at having got her drunken charge up to the porch, Desi felt disgusted. "And you have to ask why she ran out?"

"But—"

She cut him off, too angry to listen to his crazy explanation. "Where's the key?"

"Key?"

"To the house."

Slowly, hoping to penetrate his beer-fogged brain she asked slowly, "Where are your house keys?"

"In my pocket." He vaguely gestured with his beer toward his hips.

"Could you get them out?" she asked.

Seth shook his head. "I might spill my beer if I try. You get them out."

"I'm not reaching in your pant's pocket."

No way was she sticking her hand down this drunken, jilted groom's pants. Why on earth had she wasted her high school years mooning over Seth Rutherford?

Back then she'd put him on a pedestal. But today, she was a little disappointed in him—disappointed that he'd been willing to marry for less than true love.

Desi might be a romantic, but she believed that love mattered.

She put aside thoughts of disappointment and love, and simply concentrated on the task at hand—to get to Seth's keys and get him safely in his house.

Engaging Styles might use *There's Nothing We Can't Handle* for a company motto, but when she'd come up with the idea she'd never imagined a situation quite like this. Catching the groom before he fell over was enough of a challenge. She wasn't pocket surfing for keys, too.

"You've got a dirty mind Desi. Dirty-minded Desi. Dainty, dirty-minded Desi. D—"

"Get the keys," she said.

"They're in my jacket pocket." He jiggled his left shoulder.

"Oh." Desi retrieved the keys from his jacket. Anything to get him in the house.

She unlocked the door and Seth didn't wait for her to help him, he practically bounded into the house.

Drunken men would do well to remember that thresholds were not level with porches, she thought as his bound turned into a fall, right onto the slate entryway floor and right onto a rather irate cat. His beer splatted against the slate, hitting both Seth and the cat.

"Mreow," the cat cried and started hissing at Seth's prostrate form.

"Sorry, Schrodinger," Seth muttered.

Schrodinger the cat stalked from the room, apparently not willing to accept Seth's apology.

Desi stared at the crumpled mass on the floor. The only thing that kept her from kicking him was a sense of pity, despite what she'd said. A man whose bride had run out on the wedding deserved at least a bit of compassion.

"Come on, Seth, let's get you to bed," she said.

"I can't go to bed with you, even if you have totally waste-free breasts. I'm not that kind of a guy." With that, he simply lay on the floor and closed his eyes.

"Seth, come on. You can't sleep here."

"Sure I can." He curled into a little ball, and pillowed his head on his elbow.

"You've got to get up." Desi tried to pull him, but he didn't budge. She dropped his arm. She wasn't going to be able to get this guy on his feet until he wanted to get on his feet. And it didn't appear he wanted to.

Darn. Now what?

Desi sank on the floor across from Seth's prostrate form. She glanced through the doorway into his living room. There wasn't much to look at. It was functional and orderly. She doubted she'd find even a stray crumb in his couch cushions.

The foyer light illuminated the room. It wasn't enough to tell if there was any color on his walls, but she doubted it. It was probably plain, neutral white. No imagination or passion anywhere.

Seth's cat crept cautiously onto her lap. She stroked the ugly tabby's damp fur.

"You okay, Schrodinger?" She couldn't resist smiling at the cat's name.

There was a twentieth century physicist who'd come up with a theory called *Schrodinger's Cat*. Okay, so it was an odd sort of humor. Certainly not something most people outside the field of science would get. But she got it and she liked it.

Desi wasn't sure why Seth's quiet sense of humor pleased her, but it did.

She looked at him. His blond hair—which would be more at home on a beach-boy than a stodgy professor—spilled over his forehead. Gently, she pushed a stray lock back in place.

She hated leaving him lying on the floor, but Seth Rutherford wasn't her concern. She'd seen to it that he made it home safe and her job was officially done.

She could leave now and forget all about him.

CHAPTER TWO

There was only one rule for Wednesday night dinners at Hazard's—men weren't invited.

Desi took a large bite of her four-cheese lasagna, savoring every fat-producing calorie.

Mary Jo Mills, Pam Steele and Desi met at Hazard's down on the bay every Wednesday night for dinner. The food was out of this world and the restaurant's deck was situated right on the bayfront walkway.

Mary Jo, Pam, and Desi. They'd been friends since high school. Actually, they'd been more than friends, they'd been sisters.

Mary Jo was the girl Desi's parents had always wished they had. A professional and a mother. She worked as a chemist and balanced four kids and a husband.

Pam taught music and was as single as Desi. She said music was easier to figure out than men...but that didn't stop her from trying.

Their interests were different, but their friendship was strong, even after all these years.

"So, how was last weekend's wedding?" Mary Jo asked.

"The wedding was a disaster," Desi moaned.

"Oh, no. What happened?" Pam glanced at a man in a business suit and whispered, "Silk boxers at three o'clock."

Mary Jo and Desi both stole a glance at the James-Bond-wannabe and nodded agreement.

Desi answered, "A runaway bride. I've never lost a bride before. Phil wanted to tackle her, but I wasn't quite sure what to do."

"I'm assuming she ran before the I-do's?" Mary Jo asked as she sipped on her margarita.

"Oh, yeah. Left the groom standing at the altar. She seemed nice enough when I worked with her planning the wedding. Well, I didn't exactly plan it with her, but with her mother and sister. They seemed to run the show. But she still seemed nice. Maybe she was a little more nervous than most brides. But no matter what, running out on the wedding? No one should be left at the altar like that. Part of me wanted to let Phil tackle her. I felt so bad for the groom."

"Oh, the poor man. Was he cute? Maybe you should introduce us and I can comfort him," Pam said.

The idea of Pam comforting Seth didn't sit well.

"Cute?" Desi repeated.

She knew she could rhapsodize on just how cute he was. She'd done it often enough in high school. This was the perfect opportunity to mention the groom was Seth Rutherford. Given the intensity of her schoolgirl crush, she was pretty sure Pam and Mary Jo would remember him.

But Desi didn't mention knowing him or her schoolgirl crush on him. She knew Pam and Mary Jo would make a big deal about it, would want every tiny detail. And she could imagine what they'd say about her driving him home. No, if she didn't want to think about Seth Rutherford, she certainly didn't want to talk about him. And since there was nothing to tell, mentioning him would be unnecessary.

So, instead of telling them the groom was Seth, she spotted a middle-aged man sporting an earring and wearing clothes that would look more at home on a twenty-year-old and picked up their game. "Silk bikini underwear. He's trying to prove something."

"It's not working," Pam said with a laugh. "I like guys who are more comfortable with who they are. Who don't have anything to prove." She scanned the crowd and pointed to a thirty-ish man wearing jeans and a rugby shirt. "Now, take Mr. Rugby for instance. He looks very comfortable with who he is."

"Boxers," Desi said. "Cotton boxers. Bet he has some funny ones in his drawer. Heck, a guy like that would even wear the kind with little pink hearts on them. To him, they're just underwear."

"Dare me to ask what he has on tonight?" Pam asked.

"Pam, behave," Mary Jo scolded in a mommish voice.

"There was a time you'd have been the one asking him," Pam said.

"But that was before I got married. Happily married to a perfect man. Speaking of men—" Mary Jo started.

Pam interrupted. "That does seem to be what we talk about the most on Wednesdays, have you noticed? Talking about them, watching them … What is it about men that makes for such fascinating discussions? Your deserted groom, for instance, Desi. I could spend an entire evening talking about him. My heart goes out to him. Tell us more. What did you do after the bride left? What did he do?"

"There's not much to tell. He was a good sport and invited everyone to the reception since it was paid for."

"That's classy," Pam said. "I like classy."

"So how was your week?" Desi asked Mary Jo. She was anxious to turn the conversation from Seth.

"My week? It was hellish enough to make my mother feel vindicated that her curse—you know, the one where she said, *someday I hope you have kids who behave just like you*—worked," Mary Jo said picking up the conversation, just like Desi had hoped she would.

"The kids were in rare form," she continued. "I swear to Pete, one of these days someone is going to turn us in for breaking some sort of noise ordinance. Let's see the injuries of the week included one human bite, one bruised knee, and a brush burn. But the big news is Paulie got a call from a girl. He…"

Mary Jo started entertaining Pam and Desi with her kids' exploits, and though Desi made an attempt to follow the conversation, she couldn't help but think about Seth.

She'd spent a great deal of time thinking about him since Saturday. She wasn't sure why, other than she felt bad for him.

Mary Jo talked about her son's call from a girl and Desi couldn't help but remember that one time she'd called Seth's house. Thank goodness it had been before the days of Caller ID.

She'd dialed, fully intending to ask Seth to the Spring Fling dance. His mother had answered. "Hello?"

Desi had sat there, trying to catch her rapidly fleeing breath. Inhale, exhale. Inhale, exhale.

"Well, I never. How dare you call and breathe in my ear!" Seth's mother had exclaimed right before she hung up on Desi.

Desi lost her nerve and didn't call back.

What would have happened if she'd found the courage to ask for him and asked him out?

She'd never know and that was probably a good thing. Some things were better left in the realm of fantasy. She had a feeling her girlhood crush on Seth Rutherford was one of them.

"But Paulie's phone call wasn't the highlight of the week. My flowers were."

"Flowers?" Pam asked.

"A dozen roses." Mary Jo looked a little misty as she took a sip of her drink. "The card said, *You're beautiful.* Isn't that the most romantic thing?"

Mary Jo and her husband, Paul, were Desi's relationship role models. They worked together in the same lab. They shared a family and still had an incredible, romantic passion for each other. Why, he even sent her flowers saying he still though she was beautiful. That was romantic. It made Desi's heart melt a little, thinking of their true fairytale romance.

That's what Desi wanted. A man who would still send her flowers and think she was beautiful after years of marriage. A man who shared her passions and whose passions she could share. A true, enduring romance.

A prince charming sort of guy who would carry her off into the sunset and wake up next to her for the rest of her sunrises.

"Oh, my gosh," Pam whispered pointing at a man who'd taken a seat at the bar. "I don't think it matters what sort of underwear that one chooses. He's the type who only makes me wonder one thing...how long would it take to get him out of his underwear?"

Mary Jo snorted margarita out her nose as she laughed.

Desi looked at the man. Sure he was hot, but not as hot as Seth.

She stifled a groan, not wanting to alert her friends.

She had to stop thinking about Seth.

She shook her head and forced herself to study the man at the bar. "Thong. Definitely a thong underwear. If he doesn't wear one, he should."

Mary Jo and Pam tore their gazes away from Mr. Thong, took one look at Desi and all three women started laughing.

Desi forced herself to concentrate on dinner. She wasn't going to think about Seth Rutherford any more.

She'd outgrown her girlhood infatuation years ago, she reminded herself.

There was a question that kept niggling at her thoughts, though. Could she outgrow her adult attraction to him?

"Forget it, Phil. You can't just walk out."

Desi glanced at her watch. It was already after three on Friday afternoon. There was no time left to find someone to replace Phil before the Mentz wedding this evening and there was no way she alone could handle the thousand and one details that needed to be handled.

Phil wasn't full-time. During the weekdays she was on her own, but at the actual weddings, she needed someone to help coordinate all the details.

No way was he walking out on her now. She was going to tell him so. She was going to put her foot down and insist he live up to his obligations.

"Phil, you just can't—"

"Desi, this is the job I've been waiting for. The one in Atlanta."

Atlanta.

That magic word that stopped any further protests.

Desi's heart turned to mush, right then and there.

Atlanta.

Anywhere else in the world and she would have continued her fight with Phil. She'd berate him for leaving her in a lurch and insist he stay until she could find a replacement.

But she couldn't fight against Atlanta.

"Does she know?" Desi asked.

The *she* in question was Phil's ex-girlfriend—the girl-friend who'd accepted a job in Atlanta just three months ago after some big, mysterious fight they'd had. He wouldn't talk about it, but Desi knew he hadn't stopped thinking about it—about her.

"Not yet, but she will. My flight leaves at six. I'll have the weekend to get acclimated, and then I start work, both at the paper and on Debbie. I'm going to get her back."

How could Debbie resist a man who loved her enough to follow her?

How could Desi put up a fight against that kind of love? She couldn't.

Desi understood chasing your dreams and damning the consequences. She'd started this business against all her parent's dire warnings.

"Listen, Des," he said. "I'm really sorry. I appreciate everything you've done for me, but I can't pass up this opportunity."

"You're right," she said. "You can't. You should go after Debbie and make her see that the two of you are meant to be together."

Phil was a good friend, in addition to being a great assistant. But no matter how good an assistant he was, he was a greater guy. Debbie didn't realize how lucky she was. She had a man who'd give up everything to be with her.

"Go pack," she said. "Call or email me next week and let me know how it's going."

She could hear his sigh of relief over the phone line. "I will. Thanks for understanding, Des."

"No problem." At least it wasn't a problem for him. "I'll figure something out."

Desi hung up the phone and stared at her small, cluttered office. There was a neater office just beyond that door—soft colors and fabrics, huge overstuffed furniture that lent the room a romantic feel, she thought with more than a little bit of pride. But that was just for show, for clients. This was where she worked. It wasn't much more than a glorified broom closet, but it suited her. Desi worked best in the midst of chaos.

And she'd need to work her best to figure this out.

What was she going to do? It was late Friday afternoon and the wedding started in just an hour—she should be leaving for it right now. The reception was right after it until nine. How on earth was she going to find a replacement for Phil?

She flipped through the names in her phone book. Her parents would never lower themselves to help at a wedding. They'd never approved of her starting this business.

Desi could have talked Mary Jo into it, but Paul was out of town this weekend. That meant Mary Jo was dealing with the four kids on her own.

She paused on a page. Maybe Pam?

She dialed her friend's number.

"Hello?"

"Oh, Pam, you're there. I need you."

"Sure. Anything, you know that. What's up?"

"Any chance that you have this weekend free?"

"Well, in terms of hot dates, yes. But the students have that concert for their parents tonight—I'm on my way out now. Then it's open to the public tomorrow afternoon, remember? I mentioned it Wednesday. But what do you need? Maybe I can swing it."

But. There it was. Desi felt like the butt of some cosmic joke. "No big deal. I was a little short for a couple weddings and thought of you. You have fun at the concerts, I'll figure something out."

"You know, if it was anything but my kids..."

"I know you'd help me if you could. That's why I called. But don't worry about it. I've got other ideas. I'll see you next Wednesday."

She hung up and stared morosely at the phone.

She couldn't think of another soul who she might be able to convince to help her out in a pinch. Some favor she could collect on.

And then it hit her.

There was someone she'd been thinking about all week, though she wasn't sure why. Probably because she'd been worried about him.

He owed her. He'd said so. Giving him a transistor all those years ago might be a rather weak debt, but it was all she had. That and the fact she'd driven him home last week. Why, she'd practically saved his life. Maybe, just maybe he'd meant what he said.

And actually, it would be almost therapy. An *after-you've-been-thrown-from-a-horse-you-need-to-climb-back-on,* sort of thing.

Why, asking for help was almost a good deed. She flipped her phone book and dialed the number.

"Hello?"

Desi knew it was him. She'd recognize that voice anywhere.

She put on her professional chipper voice. "Hi, Seth. This is Desi." When he didn't say anything she added, "Desdemona Smith."

"Desi," He didn't sound overly enthusiastic. "Is something wrong?"

"It's been almost a week since … well, it's been a week. I just wanted to call and see how you were." She tapped her pen against a sheet of paper and started to doodle little circles, one on top of another.

"My life's been a comedy of errors. First Mary Kathryn left, then she called. I still don't understand, but she says we would have been miserable married, that it takes more than logic to make a marriage work. I don't know about that, but if she wouldn't have been happy, then it's a good thing we didn't go through with it. I think we're still friends. But she's not coming back to work. That might have been okay, but then our research assistant broke his arm in a freak bathtub accident and..." His voice trailed off a moment and then he said, with a sigh, "There's just so much to do."

Bathtub accident, freak or otherwise? Desi would have asked if she didn't have more pressing questions.

"I didn't mean with work, I meant, how are *you* doing?" She doodled a sketch that looked like a man's torso. *A naked man's torso.*

She took the doodle lower and realized how anatomically correct she'd just made it. Diddling with a doodle was poor form.

She scratched it out and found herself blushing. She was thankful Seth was on the other end of a phone line and not looking over her shoulder.

"I'm okay. And I'm glad you called," he said. "I want to thank you again for... well, for bringing me home before I made a total fool of myself. You promised at the rehearsal dinner that you wouldn't let me do that and you didn't. It seems every time we meet you rescue me, whether it's transistors or rides home. I'm grateful."

"I wish I could have got you into bed—" She stopped short, realizing how that sounded. "I mean, get you off the floor, but you were too heavy."

"But you covered me. That was probably more than I deserved. I'm swearing off alcohol. The whole night is pretty much a blur."

"Um, Seth. You just said you were *grateful*. I'd like to know if you're appreciative enough to reciprocate and help me out."

"Help you out?" Seth asked.

"Well, I need somebody today. I need someone desperately." There was the faintest hint of pleading in her voice, but she didn't care. Desi knew she did need Seth Rutherford and she needed him desperately.

Seth gulped convulsively.

Desi couldn't mean what he thought she meant. She didn't need him like *that*, so he didn't tell her that one of the most vivid recollections he had from his almost-wedding night was Desi's *assets* rubbing against him in the car.

He wasn't sure why they were rubbing against him and he certainly wasn't about to ask, but he distinctly remembered her breasts and that led to quite a bit of *need* on his part too.

"Desperately?" he simply asked, waiting for her to clarify what it was she needed because he knew it wasn't him. He didn't seem to inspire that sort of need in women. At least not in Mary Kathryn and probably not in Desi either.

"Oh, you don't know the half of it. I can't think of anyone who would do it but you."

Seth didn't want to tell her that he'd been thinking of her as well. That didn't seem like what a jilted groom should be thinking about. "Uh, maybe we should talk about this *need*."

"Oh, there's no time to talk. It's really just a matter of being able to follow directions. And since you're into science, I'm sure you can follow along."

"You're going to direct me?"

"Of course. I mean, I'm sure you shine in the lab and even in the classroom, but I don't think you're as experienced as I am at this kind of stuff."

Had he, in his drunkenness, told her that he and Mary Kathryn had never made love?

If he told her, he hoped he'd explained that he was more than capable of making love.

He hoped he'd told her that it was just that Mary Kathryn had always seemed like a friend—just a friend—and it was especially hard to get all hot and bothered by a goggle-wearing, lab-sharing friend. He just figured he'd get hot and bothered after the wedding.

But he'd reassessed that postulate since the almost-wedding. Chemistry alone might not be enough to base a relationship on—he still believed common interests and goals were the most important ingredients—but hot and bothered should be *part* of a relationship.

Maybe if he and Mary Kathryn had experienced more elemental reactions to each other, she wouldn't have left.

But now there was no wedding and no marriage, so he didn't have to worry about getting hot and bothered in the least by Mary Kathryn.

But Desi... now that was another story all together.

Not that he was hot and bothered. Maybe he suspected he could get hot and bothered about her, not that he would. He was swearing off women.

"Seth, I know it's asking a lot, but I truly do need you. You said your research assistant was injured and you're swamped. Well, I'll even help you out in return if you like, sort of a tit-for-tat thing."

Her phrasing reminded him of his need and left him grateful she was a phone-line away at the moment, and not near enough to notice that she wasn't the only needy person in this conversation.

"I know you're not used to being bossed around," she continued, "so I promise I'll be gentle."

"I'll do I,!" he said, though he wasn't sure what he was agreeing to and was even less sure why he was agreeing to it in the first place.

"You will? Great. I'll explain everything when you get there. St. John's on East Twenty-Sixth Street. I need you there in an hour."

"We're going to do it in a Church?"

"Of course. I admit, I've done it other places. Some of them were almost bizarre. I mean, the beach makes sense, but there was one time we did it in the middle of the Mall. Why would anyone want to do it there?"

"In the Mall?" He gulped convulsively. "In the middle of the Mall?"

"I'll tell you all my stories, if you like. Just be at St. John's in an hour. Oh, and do you own a tux?"

"A tux?" he asked.

"Never mind, I'll take care of it. Thanks, Seth. I owe you. Bye."

Seth sat, feeling shell-shocked, as he listened to the dial tone buzzing in his ear. What on earth had he just agreed to?

It had to have something to do with her job. She worked in churches. He was sure he hadn't agreed to what he thought he'd agreed to. And maybe he felt a little disappointed that he hadn't. Because if he had agreed to what he originally thought he was agreeing to, he'd be the one who'd owe Desi.

He'd owe her big.

CHAPTER THREE

Desi was in big trouble if Seth didn't arrive soon.
She glanced out the church door for the hundredth
time. Where was he?

Maybe Seth had reconsidered and wasn't going to show.

She groaned at the thought. Well, she'd just have to
muddle through the wedding without an assistant, if that
was the case. She'd just have to figure out how to be in two
places at once.

No problem. She could handle it.

She looked at her watch again. She'd wait another
couple minutes and then she'd have to get started without him.

A neon-yellow sports car shot passed the church and
parked down the block. A man climbed out of it.

A man with sandy blond hair who looked like Seth from
a distance. But it couldn't be Seth. Seth was a stodgy, pro-
fessorly sort who should drive a practical car, not a sporty,
neon-yellow two-seated babe-magnet.

No, Seth wasn't some blond boy-toy driving a car guar-
anteed to make women drool.

The boy-toy came closer.

It *was* Seth.

Desi let out a long breath she hadn't realized she'd been
holding.

"Hi," he called as he started up the long flight of stairs that led to the front doors of the old church.

"Seth." Desi couldn't remember when she'd been so happy to see someone. She assured herself that she was only happy to see him though because she needed his help, not for any other reason. "Nice car."

"Do you like it?" he asked.

"Of course. What's not to like?"

She could almost imagine sitting in the passenger seat, the wind blowing through her hair, the car's engine purring as they rode down the interstate going somewhere, anywhere.

"It's a great car," she said, though she was still rather caught up in her mental picture of riding in the car.

"I bought it this week. I wanted to do something wild. Something out of character. This was the best I could come up with." He smiled a lopsided smile.

Desi suddenly realized that in her fantasy-ride, Seth was the one driving.

She had to get control of herself. Despite the awesome car and the lopsided grin with accompanying dimple, Seth wasn't Desi's type.

Or was he?

She wasn't precisely sure what her type was, come to think of it. It wasn't as if she wasn't looking, but she never seemed to find her prince charming and Desi wasn't going to settle for less than her perfect man. And she certainly wasn't going to settle for less than love.

She glanced up at Seth and for a moment tried to imagine he was the prince she'd been waiting for. She imagined him climbing off his pearly white steed, wearing a regal looking cloak and crown as he whispered the sweet words she'd waited her whole life to hear—

The mental-image popped like a balloon, and instead of a prince, her imaginary Seth was wearing a lab coat and shaking a finger in her face as he said, *"Love isn't logical and I like logic."*

Desi shook her head, trying to clear the daydream.

"Come on, we need to hurry," she said as she led Seth into the church and down the stairs to the restroom.

No more fantasies today. She had a wedding to run.

"Here." She handed him the tux. "Go change in the bathroom. It might be a little off, but I think I came close on the size."

"You never told me exactly why I was here. I mean, we're not getting married, are we? You remember the last time I tried that. It didn't go so well." He paused a moment, and added, "You didn't say just what you needed me for."

"My assistant quit and I need someone to help me."

"Help you with ...?"

"The wedding. The Mentz wedding." She gave him a little shove into the bathroom. "Hurry up and change. It's already started and I like to watch."

A few minutes later he came out wearing the tux. It fit as if it had been made for him. He held out the tie. "Would you mind?"

Desi did mind.

She minded a lot.

She didn't want to get any closer to Seth than she had to. She wasn't sure what to make of this man who one minute was throwing beer on his cat and the next minute he was driving a sports car and looking yummy in a tux. She didn't want to get any closer to this man who invaded her fantasies.

She glanced at her watch and knew there was nothing to do but tie his tie. So she took it from him and quivered as her fingers brushed his.

The church must be drafty. That was the reason for the chills that ran up her spine, she assured herself as she took a step closer and wrapped the tie around his neck.

She ignored the fact that Seth smelled good. Not in a I-used-half-a-bottle-of-cologne sort of way but in a I-smell-like-a-man sort of way.

She held her breath and tried not to notice, as she made short work of tying the tie. She took a step back, exhaled and inhaled deeply, and admired her handiwork.

"You'll do," she said. "Let's go. We're running late."

She led him back up the stairs and they snuck quietly into the sanctuary of the Church. "We'll sit back here until just before the end of the service."

"Then what?" he whispered.

"Don't you worry, all you have to do is follow directions."

Seth had been right when he'd known he was wrong. On the drive over to the church he figured whatever Desi needed him for had to do with a wedding.

She was a wedding coordinator and needed him at a church.

Yes, it didn't take a keen intellect to reach the conclusion that she needed him for something wedding-ish, but that didn't stop the idea of her needing something more from crossing his mind.

That he wished Desi wanted him in a carnal-way instead of a business-way left him feeling confused. After all, his entire relationship with Mary Kathryn had been built on common work interests, as well as mutual admiration and respect. It wasn't this chemical sort of attraction he felt for Desi.

The idea of Desi merely wanting him was an appealing thing on some basic level, but basic was all it was. It wasn't as if he really knew her. This attraction was a hormonal thing. Women weren't the only ones who were sometimes at the mercy of them. It was perfectly natural to be attracted to a gorgeous woman.

Gorgeous. Oh, yeah, that was the right word to describe Desi.

He glanced at her, sitting next to him but not touching him. She was wearing a navy blue dress. Not too businessy, but not overly dressy. It hung to her knees and was—*demure*, that was a good word for it. It was sort of shimmery and soft looking. He didn't know much about fabrics, but he'd bet it was silk.

Her hair fascinated him. As soft and silky looking as the dress. He had an urge to reach out and just run his fingers through it. He wanted to do something more wild and out of character than buying a sports car—and specifically, he wanted to do it with this woman. But he kept his hands firmly in his lap.

Yes, Desi was gorgeous, but that being said, he didn't really know her. Oh, he knew she was generous. All those years ago she'd proven that by helping him win the science fair. She'd proved it again by helping him home. But beautiful and generous weren't enough to form an attraction, at least not for him.

He wanted a partner, someone who shared his interests, not just someone to share his bed.

And yet…

As he studied her, Desi sniffed, pulling his attention from shimmery dresses to the tissue she dabbed her eyes.

"You're crying," he whispered.

"I cry at everything from commercials to sad country songs," she whispered back and punctuated the sentence with another sniff. "I cried when you won that science award. And as much as other things make me cry, weddings are the worst. I always end up bawling."

"Why?"

"Because they're so romantic. They're two people standing in front of their friends and family and declaring that they're going to spend the rest of their lives loving each other."

"If you believe that, then why are you crying? That shouldn't make you sad."

"I'm not sad, I'm happy. Happy they're going to have happily-ever-after. And happy that I had a hand in making this a special day."

"That's a lot of happys for something that probably won't last. Marriages needed to be based on more than emotional nonsense."

He thought of his mother and father's relationship, full of emotions run amuck. Volatile, that was the word for it. They fought with as much passion as they loved. And they wore those feelings on their sleeves—bubbling, fuming, fighting, loving.

Something a little less capricious would certainly be preferable.

"Look at the statistics" he continued. "If love did indeed mean a fairytale endings, then there wouldn't be so many divorces. Logic. Compatibility. Common goals. Those are things that a marriage should be based on. Those are things that will make a relationship work long after the initial emotional, chemical response has faded into a distant memory."

He'd based his relationship with Mary Kathryn on that premise. It was a sound theory.

Then why hadn't it work out?

He hadn't made it beyond the engagement. But why?

That was the question no amount of scientific research could answer.

Desi just shot him a dirty look and then turned her attention to the ceremony.

"I'd like to introduce Mr. and Mrs. Mark Mentz," the priest said as the ceremony ended. The guests stood and applauded.

"Come on," Desi said. She led him into the church's foyer.

"What now?" he asked, wondering why he'd said yes in the first place.

"Remind me to debate what marriages should be based on later. Right now, we're on. I'm going to stay here and take care of the reception line, and then get the pictures started."

She dug through her briefcase and handed a couple sheets of crumpled paper to Seth. "Here. Do you know where the Siebenbuerger Club is?"

Seth took the mangled looking papers. "What are these?"

"That one's the seating chart, this one's," she indicated an even rattier looking sheet of paper, "is the checklist. I need you to head over to the club. Make sure they have everything set up, that the candles are lit and ... well, its all there. Then, as people come in, help them find their table. I know you can follow the chart. I'll join you as soon as possible."

"I need a clipboard," he muttered. He needed to put her messy notes into some order. He smoothed them, but it didn't help.

How could she work like this? He thought of his own orderly system. Desi could use some pointers on neat, orderly charts.

"Pardon?" she asked.

"I need a clipboard, something to organize all this. I need to get it all straight so I can think."

"Think about what?"

36

"About...just get me a clipboard. I can't work like this," he said, turning over the crumbled mass of paper in his hands.

"Seth, I don't have time to get you a clipboard. I just need you to take care of this. It's all written down. No problem."

"But—"

"It's all on the lists," she said, her voice tinged with exasperation. It didn't take a scientist to analyze her frustration level. "You don't need a clipboard. How hard can it be?"

How hard could it be?

Seth looked at the mangled papers Desi had thrust at him. How hard could it be to fold a paper in half, neatly and evenly? Obviously too hard for Desi.

"Fine," he said. He could meet this challenge. He'd not only meet it, he'd surpass it. He'd show her how to be organized. "I'll take care of everything. You won't be long?"

"I'll be there as soon as I can."

The Siebenbuerger Club was only a few blocks from St. Johns, so Seth arrived within minutes. He parked his car in the lot across the street and walked toward the brick building wondering just how he'd become an assistant—a wedding coordinator's assistant.

Another wedding reception.

How had it happened? The only good thing was that this time he wasn't the jilted-groom, but the go-fer.

He plodded into the club, wishing he was anywhere but here. A doorman was checking in guests.

"I'm with the Mentz wedding," Seth said. "I'm Desi Smith's assistant. If you could show me—"

"Oh, thank goodness," the grey-haired man said. "The staff is going crazy. It seems the cake didn't arrive and they're not sure what to do."

Seth didn't know what to do about a non-existent cake either, but before he could tell the man so, he found himself hustled down a hall to a small office.

"Are you from the Mentz wedding?" a rather frazzled looking dark-haired woman asked.

"Yes," Seth said, tentatively.

"Here." She handed him the phone. "It's the bakery. Dealing with cakes isn't my job. I'm just the caterer."

It wasn't his job either. What did he know about wedding cakes, other than his almost-mother-in-law had thought his was too small last week?

Seth longed for his quiet office. Books and mussels. Heck, though the science was more his thing than the classes, he'd even prefer a lecture hall full of college kids right now.

At eight am.

On a Monday morning.

But since he knew nothing was going to save him at this point, he put the phone to his ear. "Now, what's the problem?"

"There is no problem I can't handle."

Desi murmured the phrase over and over. It was her own private mantra.

She was going to kill Seth Rutherford, PH.D.

Pretty Hideously Dead. That's what the initials should stand for. A slow, agonizing death, that's what he was in for when she found him.

He taught science, for pity's sake. Surely he could follow simple instructions? She's written everything down for him. And yet, as she walked into the reception hall, the candles weren't lit, there were no hors d'oeuvres set out, and there was no Seth pointing guests to their tables.

There was no Seth period.

She watched people mill around, reading nameplates, looking for their seats.

As she rushed into action making sure the caterer started serving, that the bartender was ready, that somebody lit the candles, and that people found their tables, she thought of new, horrible ways to torture the fink.

She would—

"You're here!" Seth, the man doomed to die a painful death as soon as this reception was over, said as he rushed into the room. His tux rumpled and smeared with dirt. There was something in his hair.

Not only was he late, he was a mess. She was going to have to pay extra to get that tux cleaned.

"I'm here, but where were you?" Desi said sharply and then continued without allowing him time to answer. "Nothing's ready. The bridal party will be here in a few minutes and nothing's done. I called you today because I was desperate, I needed you and—"

He interrupted her. "You also needed a cake."

"Pardon?"

"The cake wasn't here. The bakery's van broke down on I-90 and the tow truck was coming, so I shot out of here to get it. If I hadn't, it would have been too late by the time the bakery driver arranged other transportation. You'd have had a reception and no cake."

"Oh, Seth, I take back every wicked thing I thought about you. I'm so sorry. I—"

"Uh, don't be too thankful just yet. It's a big cake. There were five boxes, and then there was all the little fountain and column stuff, and, well you saw my new car, it's only got two seats and not much of a trunk."

"So you don't have it?"

"Oh, the cake is fine. It's the bride and groom. I was driving uncharacteristically fast and I'm afraid they're gone."

"The bride and groom?" He'd hit her newly married couple? Desi turned ready to rush to the parking lot and save her clients, but Seth caught her.

"Not the real bride and groom. The cake bride and groom. They're somewhere on Old French Road. I filled up the trunk with the columns and the fountain. Then I took down the top of the car, and stacked everything. I sort of belted all the boxes in place in the passenger seat, and they were pretty secure.

"Generally I drive slow, but I knew that you needed me here, so I was going a little faster than I should have. So when this truck in front of me slammed on his brakes, so did I. The bride and groom were riding on the top of the boxes and they flew out of the car. I spent fifteen minutes looking for them, but it was on the part of Old French with the steep incline, and I think they're in the creek and half way to Lake Erie by now. I'm sorry."

"I—"

Whatever she was going to say was cut short by the videographer interrupting them. "Desi, where's Phil? I need his help with this," he held his camcorder out. "It's—"

"Listen, Desi, you've got your hands full. I'll figure out putting the cake together. Trust me," Seth said.

Certain that she was going to regret it later, Desi gave a small nod. "Okay, but don't ruin it."

CHAPTER FOUR

Ruined.

Well and truly wrecked.

Her career was over.

Desi Smith knew the truth when it stared her in the face. In one short evening Seth Rutherford had completely obliterated her business reputation. She'd never get another job. She'd be forced to work for someone else.

Another thought occurred to her.

It was horrible.

If her parents found out that *Engaging Styles* had failed, they'd renew their efforts to get her into a *real* job. A professional job. A nine-to-five job.

She hiccupped again.

She'd been hiccupping ever since Seth had destroyed her business. Not just ordinary hiccups.

No.

Hers were body-wracking hiccups. Everyone dealt with stress in their own way. Though given her druthers, she'd never have chosen this particular way. She dealt with stress by hiccupping.

Last time she'd got them this bad she'd just stood up to her parents—finally refusing to go to grad school. She'd told them about her dream job and they hadn't taken it well.

The resulting confrontation had led to hiccups that were so bad she'd had to go to the doctor's for a shot.

When she got them like this they could last for days. The shots cleared them up, but she hated shots. Thinking about getting one made her even more nervous and she let out a long string of hiccups.

"I'm so sorry about everything," Seth said for at least the hundredth time.

He'd insisted on driving her to her apartment and Desi hadn't been able to put together enough words between the hiccupping to argue.

Hiccup, was her only response. Her diaphragm was already aching.

"At least the cake turned out nice," he said. "Well, until I sat in it."

Nice? Seth had obviously not seen many elaborate tiered wedding cakes. His finished product resembled *The Leaning Tower of Pisa*.

Or closer to the point, a Salvador Dali painting. Surreal and leaning every which way.

Hiccup.

"And the bride and groom. They were pure inspiration," he said, trying to cheer her up.

"They were—*hiccup*—Barbie dolls, Seth."

"But getting the bride's niece to lend them to me, well, it cost me five bucks. And then she said I ruined them at the end so that was another thirty dollars to replace them. Though I don't think frosting ruins dolls. And I'm going to check and see if Barbie's really cost that much. I think I got suckered."

"I know you—*hiccup*—were trying to—*hiccup*—help and the cake—*hiccup*—problems weren't really your fault—*hiccup*—and the dolls were sort of cute. But…" she let the sentence trail off and had a loud series of hiccups.

"I know, I know, I shouldn't have lectured that lady about sexual harassment, but come on, Desi, she pinched my butt."

"That's not what I—*hiccup*—was talking about either—*hiccup*—and you know it." She hiccupped and said, "I'm ruined. Done in—*hiccup*—by a mad-scientist and a wedding cake."

Seth glanced her way and the wind caught his blond hair, messing it slightly. He gave her an apologetic look. "You're right. I know what you're talking about. It's just that there it was, that garter, flying right at me, and the last thing in the world I want is another wedding, so I backed away, hoping that kid with the glasses would catch it and I forgot about the cake."

"No one else—*hiccup*—ever will. I'm ruined."

She'd worked so hard for the last few years. She'd defied her parents and followed her dream. *Engaging Styles* was that dream and because of Seth it had now turned into a nightmare.

"Desi, I don't think it's the end of your career. After all, you didn't sit in the wedding cake. I did."

"You were working for me." She hiccupped again. "I should have driven myself home. I'm perfectly—*hiccup*—capable—*hiccup*—of—*hiccup*—driving."

"Desi, you'd end up in an accident. You're upset and it's my fault," he said and then added, "Plus I owed you a ride. Friends don't let friends drive drunk or while under the influence of near-terminal-hiccups."

He pulled up to the address she'd given him and parked in the lot. "Come on, let me take you in."

"I can—*hiccup*—get in myself."

He opened his door, walked around the car and opened hers. "Still, I'm going to see you to your door. It's dark and I'm not letting you go up yourself."

He offered her his hand, but Desi ignored it. "Fine."

They took the elevator to the second floor and Desi morosely led Seth to her apartment.

"Desi," came a cry. And Desi didn't have to be a scientist to know that Murphy's Law was being applied in full force tonight.

Her parents were here. Standing in the hall. Waiting.

Oh, no, they found out about the date with Stanley… or rather the date she'd broken with him.

Stanley, an up-and-coming banker who her parents thought would be perfect for her.

And he would be… if she was looking for a man who couldn't pass a mirror without preening. A man who left a fifteen percent-to-the-penny tip for the waiter at their one-and-only dinner. She just couldn't face going out with him again and after breaking a second date, she'd dodged his calls, but obviously couldn't dodge her parents, since they were standing right outside her apartment door.

"Mom and Dad—*hiccup*. What's up?" she asked, playing innocent.

Desi looked at her parents and tried to see them through Seth's eyes.

They looked harmless enough.

Her mother, Barbara, was petite, her dark hair highlighted with striking streaks of grey and vivid blue eyes that defied age. Her father, Verle, was much taller than Seth. His hair was completely grey with no signs of thinning at all.

"Your mother wanted to talk to you about Stanley. He called, upset that you'd broken your date. He'd been so excited about your first date and says he hasn't been able to get a hold of you to reschedule the second one. We said we'd help and were just about to let ourselves into the apartment to wait for you. And who is this?" Her father eyed Seth suspiciously.

"Seth. Seth Rutherford." He held out his hand and the men shook. "I'm filling in as Desi's assistant tonight."

Desi unlocked the apartment door and let in all her uninvited guests.

"*Hiccup.*" She led them into her living room with its rose-colored walls, lace curtains, floral printed fabrics. Normally walking into her living room was the biggest pleasure of her day. She loved the room. But today all she wanted was to walk straight through her living room and into her bedroom where she could climb beneath the covers and hide for the next week or so.

She glanced at her three uninvited guests and knew there was no escape.

"Mom, Dad, this is Seth—we went to school together—and Seth, this is my mother and father, Verle and Barbara Smith." An uncontrollable series of hiccups punctuated her introductions.

Rather than address Seth with social pleasantries, her mother turned to Desi and asked, "Where's Phil?"

Desi couldn't seem to get a word out between the hiccups, and finally Seth answered, "I volunteered to fill in for him."

"So you're not a wedding consultant by trade and not Desi's date?" Her mother was staring at Seth as if he were a specimen under her microscope.

Don't say it, Desi willed. *Please don't say it.* She'd forgive him for ruining her career if only he didn't tell them—

"No to both. I'm a professor of Biology and Desi and I are just friends."

He said it. A professional who worked at a real profession.

He could have said male-escort or tarot card reader. How about rodeo rider? Anything but a professional.

Darn.

Her mother was eying Seth up in a most uncomfortable way, even as her father said, "If Seth is just a friend, then there's no reason you can't go out with Stanley again."

No reason except he had the personality of a parsnip. No, make that a mushroom. Fungus. That was how she'd describe Stanley Stall. Her parents had just *happened* to invite him to dinner last week on the same night they happened to invite Desi. She'd gone out with him once after that, and once was enough.

"You broke your dinner date with him Tuesday, then he asked you to go to a movie on Wednesday and that you *said* you were busy." Her mother placed just enough emphasis on the said part that Desi knew that her mother knew she'd lied to Stanley.

"Sorry, Mom. You know, I always have dinner with Mary Jo and Pam on Wednesdays. And I don't really have any nights open soon. With Phil gone I'm going to be busier than usual." And—even with her now doomed career—she was unlikely to get un-busy ever again, at least for Stanley.

Her parents acted as a unit. They used to push her toward a career worthy of her intellect, both acting in tandem. They dreamed of Nobel Prizes and academic honors. When that didn't work, they started pushing her toward men.

Suitable men.

Unfortunately their idea of a man who would suit Desi was about as accurate as their opinion of a career that would suit her.

Desi might not know what she was looking for in a man, but it obviously wasn't what her parents were looking for.

Her mother shot Desi a look that said they weren't finished discussing Stanley, then turned to Seth and said, "So tell us, Seth, what exactly do you do?"

"I'm studying the impact of foreign invaders on the lake's ecosystem—"

"I'm going to change," Desi said, though her parents didn't even hear her. Seth did. He looked at her helplessly as her mother led him toward the couch.

Desi walked toward her bedroom, but could hear her mother grilling him about his teaching and his research. Desi took off her dress, stripping down to her lacy underwear, then pulled on jeans and a t-shirt over her hiccup-aching torso.

Desi had been stressed before her parents arrived, but now? She might not ever recover.

She hurried back out to the living room.

"...and Desi's in Mensa. Did you know that? She was in the gifted program in school. She got a full academic scholarship to college. And what is she doing with her life? Planning weddings, that's what."

Seth said, "I don't know—"

"Neither do I," her mother said. "Why look how she broke the date off with Stanley. He's a perfectly respectable, successful man. I love my daughter, but I don't understand her."

"I think you're missing the big picture here," Seth said. "Desi isn't wasting her talents at all. She's very talented at what she does. I've got letters behind my name, but I couldn't do what she does. I ruined everything she worked so hard at in just one short evening."

"But she could be anything she wanted," her mother insisted.

"And that's just what she's doing. Finding something you love doing, something you're good at doing, and then doing it. That's a success in my book."

Desi heard the words and realized that she hadn't hiccupped once as she blatantly eavesdropped. Seth had just stood up to her mother on her behalf.

He was a hero.

Suddenly Desi forgot his every mishap.

"Well, I guess I never thought about it that way," her mother said slowly.

"You should. I wish I could find a way for all my students to discover what it is they would love to do with their lives. I know I'm a better researcher than an instructor, but teaching is part of the package and I do my best to inspire them to do just what your daughter has done. I encourage them to find their passion."

He paused a moment and said, "Watching Desi in action I learned that she handles a million different details flawlessly and seemingly effortlessly. It isn't as easy as she makes it seem. I lost the bride and groom, got groped by a number of women, knocked over a stack of dishes, stepped on the bride's train, and the final icing for the evening was when I sat in the cake. I'm a total wedding disaster."

Desi's hiccups were gone for good, she realized. And she realized something else, something new about Seth Rutherford—he understood her. At least, he understood her love for what she did. And that was more than her parents had ever done.

She forgave him for his wedding disaster-itis and cleared her throat as she walked into the room.

"Desi, are you feeling better, dear?" her mother asked. Desi would have sworn there was something different in her mother's tone. Something that said she was finally beginning to understand her.

"Seth was just telling us that he doesn't think you're going to offer him a permanent job as your assistant," her father said.

Desi chuckled. "That would be an understatement. But he did try. He helped me out of a bind and even if there were a few accidents—"

Seth openly choked at her new, kinder version of his assistance.

"—I know he did his best. Did he tell you there wouldn't have even been a cake if he hadn't gone and rescued it?"

"Seth told us everything we needed to hear," her father said.

Desi shot Seth a look of gratitude.

Seth stood. "I just wanted to be sure you made it home. And now that—" Suddenly he broke off his sentence and said, "Hey, you haven't hiccupped since you came back in here."

"Like I said, I'm feeling much better."

"But I ruined your career."

"I'm sure you didn't. I'll make it up to the Mentz's somehow."

"You know, Desdemona, you could have called us, if you were desperate for help," her mother interjected.

"Not that we'd be any better at receptions than Seth here, but we would have helped you," her father added.

"You would have?" she asked, praying her jaw wasn't dragging the floor.

"Desi," her mother's voice uncharacteristically soft. "We might not understand why you chose this profession and we might have, maybe, been a little disappointed thinking you weren't making the most of your intellect, but Seth reminded us that you are following your heart. He reminded us that you are good at what you do. And both your father and I respect that. But whatever you do, whatever our feelings about it, you are our daughter and if you need us, we'll always be there."

Desi's eyes misted up. She wanted to say something, but couldn't seem to find any words. "I—"

"Why don't you see Seth out," her mother said. "He's looking very uncomfortable with our little family discussion."

Wordlessly, she stood and took Seth's arm as she led him to the door.

She was touching him, she realized. She dropped his arm and stammered, "Seth, I don't know how to thank you."

She opened the door, waiting for him to leave, but he didn't. Instead, he asked, "You have another wedding tomorrow, too, don't you?"

"Yes."

"Since you couldn't have replaced Phil yet, do you still need me? I mean, if you get through this weekend, you can use next week to find someone more permanent, right?"

"Right."

"Well, I'm volunteering. Unless you'd rather ask your parents."

"I can't tell you how much their offer meant, but I suspect Mom and Dad would be less capable at assisting than you are. They're much better at running the show or giving orders."

That much was true. But what she wasn't going to say was that she wanted to see Seth again and if he helped her she knew she would.

"Fine. What time?"

Desi stared at him. If she'd followed her parent's wishes and become a scientist, Seth Rutherford would make an interesting specimen. She wasn't sure what to make of him and maybe studying him would help.

No. She took that back, she didn't want to figure him out.

Desi knew what she wanted in life—a successful career and a happily-ever-after of her own. She wanted romance. Someone who loved her to distraction and would prove it in a romance-worthy way.

She couldn't imagine Seth ever waxing poetic about his love for anyone.

No, Seth might have rescued her from her parents tonight, but he wasn't a romance hero. Add to that, he was on the rebound in a big way and you had the most unsuitable man in the whole world. She would have better luck chasing after Stanley than chasing her girlhood crush.

But that didn't stop Seth from being one of the most attractive men she'd seen in a long time.

The thought made her sigh.

"Is that *a yes, Seth, I really need you* sigh?" he asked. "Or is it a, *I'm between a rock and a hard place, so I guess I don't have a choice* sigh?"

"You're sure you want to volunteer?" she asked, hoping he'd change his mind and back out.

"I guess I am. That is, if you're not afraid to give me another try."

"Well, you didn't pass your driver's test first time, but you've managed to drive all these years without an accident, so maybe it will be the same with the wedding assistance."

"Great." He grinned.

It almost looked as if he was pleased to be helping. "What time?"

She'd let Seth help this one last time, and that would be that. They'd be even and she'd get back to normal. "Meet me at the Lutheran Church in Wesleyville about eleven, okay?"

"Why don't I pick you up a little before that and we can go together?"

"Okay."

She shut the door behind him. One more day working with Seth Rutherford and that would be it. She'd find a new assistant and get back to her life.

"Desi?" her mother called.

Speaking of getting back to, there was still the matter of Stanley to take care of.

"Coming," she called.

She glanced at the closed door.

One more day of dealing with Seth Rutherford and she'd say goodbye to the object of her teenage crush for good.

That would really be it.

CHAPTER FIVE

That was it.

Desi admitted defeat.

She couldn't sleep.

She'd tossed and turned all night long. The sun hadn't risen and she finally gave up the pretense, turned on her bedside lamp and picked up her book, *Her Perfect Man*.

Generally reading, especially reading a good romance, soothed her. But this morning non-soothing phrases kept catching her eye as she flew through the pages.

"They had everything in common."

Seth thought love should be a partnership of minds, she thought love should be a partnership of hearts.

Not that it mattered.

It wasn't as if she was considering a relationship with Seth, she told herself sternly. What she felt for him was simply a remnant of a girlhood crush.

"Romero and Cassandra fit together like two pieces of a puzzle."

Her attraction to Seth was puzzling, but she wouldn't say they fit together. She was a read-romances-in-bed sort of girl, he was a clipboard-obsessed sort of guy.

He'd spent his whole life looking for her.

Seth might have looked at her, but hadn't even noticed her in high school. Maybe he noticed a little now, but he was on the rebound, which meant that even if he were looking he wouldn't look long. Rebound relationships never lasted.

"Romero sent Cassandra chocolate… dark, rich chocolate that spoke of passion and pleasure. It was her favorite. But that came as no surprise. Romero seemed to have a sixth sense about her, as if he knew her every thought and fantasy."

Seth's idea of a fantasy was…

Desi didn't have a clue what it was. Her fantasy man would be one who knew her inside out. Even armed with a clipboard, she doubted Seth would ever figure her out.

"Romero—every woman's dream man—admitted he dreamed of her and only her."

Desi snorted. Seth probably dreamed of periodic tables.

Not that she wanted Seth to dream of her. It wasn't as if she dreamed of him. No, in order to dream she'd have to sleep and all she'd done was toss and turn.

Finally, she couldn't stand reading another word about Romero. He was perfect. Perfect for the Cassandra.

No, more than that, he was just plain perfect. Nauseatingly perfect. Heck, he'd even folded his clothes before getting into bed. He probably never left the toilet seat up and the story made no mention of him snoring.

Yeah, Desi would have liked him more if he snored. But instead, Romero was a saint.

That should make her swoon for him, instead she tossed the book on the nightstand in disgust and glanced at the clock. She needed to get ready anyway.

She took a quick shower and got ready for the day, then made her way into the kitchen for a cup of coffee. It was stupid getting so worked up over a book and Romero. He was exactly the kind of hero she was looking for, after all.

A man who shared her interests, who was romantic, who anticipated her needs and desires. A man who loved her and would do anything for her.

She pulled out the coffee and scooped heaping tablespoons into a filter, then slammed it into the coffeemaker.

Yeah, Romero was everything she was looking for in a man. A true prince charming.

She wasn't sure why that thought distressed her, but it did.

As she filled the carafe with water and dumped into the coffeemaker Seth flashed through her mind. Just a quick image of him climbing out of his banana-colored sports car.

Seth was the antithesis of what she was looking for. He was a man on the rebound, a man who didn't believe in love so much as compatibility. A man...

Oh, she had to forget about Seth Rutherford.

She should have said no last night when he offered to help at today's wedding. But she hadn't and she refused to wonder why she hadn't.

Well, she'd get through today and then she was putting all thoughts of Seth out of her mind. She was going to forget about him if it was the last thing she did.

She went to get the paper. She'd needed a heavy dose of reality after that saccharine coated Romero. She opened the door, bent to get paper, and found herself staring at shoes—well-polished, black shoes.

She looked up and there was Seth, decked out in his tux, looking totally hot.

How could she start forgetting if he looked so darned good?

"Seth?" she asked in a morning croak.

"I'm early. It's a habit. I hate to be late, so I'm always a little early."

"I was just making coffee. I need it to jump start my morning, especially my early-afternoon-wedding Saturdays. Come on in. I'll share. A quick cup and then we'll get going."

"That would be great. Are you sure you want me to help today? I mean, after yesterday..." He left the sentence hang there as he trailed after her into the kitchen.

Desi nodded at a stool, indicating he should be seated. "Sure I'm sure. I really need the help."

What was she saying?

She'd just wondered why she'd agreed to Seth's assistance today. This was the perfect opportunity to change her mind. But instead of telling him to go, she said, "You just had a few mishaps. Perfectly understandable. This is a difficult job."

She poured two cups of coffee and handed one to him, then took a seat across from him.

"You're right. This is nothing like research. Step one is always followed by step two, which is followed by step three, and then so on and so on. From what I can tell there is no order to running a wedding."

"That's because weddings are days built around emotions. And there's no telling where those emotions will take you. I mean, people passing out, over-indulging, fighting." She took a long sip and felt the caffeine surge through her system. "That's just the people stuff. Then there are wedding dresses that don't fit and you have to sew the bride into them, and missing wedding cakes—"

"Sat-in wedding cakes," he added.

Desi smiled. "Yes and the sat-in ones. It's always something. Something new, something different, and frequently something challenging. It keeps life interesting."

"Interesting is finding that the lake's clarity has increased by three percent. Interesting is following the new applications for fuel cells in automobiles. Interesting is not a plethora of over-emotional people collected in one location."

"Seth, people are what makes my job so wonderful. I mean, my parents wanted me to do something...well, like you do. But I wanted the wild emotions, the unpredictability. I wanted to be part of happily-ever-afters on a daily basis."

Seth just shook his head. "I'll help you today, but after this, I plan to go back to my rational, orderly life and forget all about weddings."

Desi looked at Seth and silently agreed. After today it was best he headed back to his lab. And she was determined that when he did she was going to forget about him as easily as he planned on forgetting about weddings.

"Forget it."

Desi knew, despite their nice conversation that morning, Seth was going to be difficult. Not that there had been any mishaps today. No, he was just being ornery.

She sometime wondered if there was some sort of gene attached to the Y chromosome that made men so...mannish. Seth had been so contrite about last night that she'd almost forgotten that he was still all man and bound to be a pain.

"It's all part of the job, Seth. And now that you're working for me—"

"This is the last day," he pointed out with a stubborn look on his face. "Next weekend you'll have a new assistant and I'll be back on the lake looking for samples, or in the lab analyzing them, or—"

"Even if it is your last day, this is part of the job and you'll have to just deal with it."

"I'm not playing stand-in-groom. The idea of being a groom, stand-in or otherwise, gives me hives. I'm not meant to be married, I've proven that. I'm mystified by the whole process of being in love. But I think the idea of smashing cake in each other's face is even more confusing than the idea of marriage."

"It's just a piece of cake." She laughed, though he didn't even crack a smile. That was one of his problems. The man had no sense of humor.

No, she took that back. He did have a small sense of humor—she'd seen it in his cat's name. But not enough to deal with cake smashing.

"Mary Kathryn and I had decided we wouldn't indulge in this arcane, insane practice." He gestured toward the beautiful five-tiered cake. "It serves no purpose."

"It's tradition." She took a mini-veil from a bag stashed underneath the cake table.

"Well, it's not a good one."

Desi set the small veil on her head, pinning it in place as she said, "It doesn't matter what you and Mary Kathryn planned, this bride and groom want it. They don't want to tempt fates by abandoning a tradition, but the bride doesn't want to mess up her makeup, so we're the stand-ins."

"Well, you're standing alone." He crossed his arms across his chest.

"Oh, no, bucko. You said you'd help me out, and this is part of it. You sat in a cake yesterday, how much more degrading could it be to have a little frosting on your face, rather than on your butt?"

She paused a moment and added, "Please?"

She was surprised at how breathy her voice was. What was it about being near Seth that sucked all the oxygen from her body? There must be a scientific explanation, but she wasn't about to ask Seth for it.

"Do you ever let up?" he asked.

"Not when there's something I want."

Want.

She could want this man. And then suddenly it hit her. There was no *could* about it. There was something about Seth Rutherford that sucked up her oxygen, that made her want to tear off his clothes and...

Cakes and weddings.

When this wedding was over she was going to forget about Seth. She was going to put aside this vestige of her girlhood crush and she definitely wasn't going to spend another sleepless night.

But first she had to get through this wedding. She had to get her mind out of the gutter and onto the job at hand. That spark of *something* she felt was nothing more than gratitude.

And this? She looked at the man standing next to her, the man who heated her blood. This was nothing more than leftover girlhood daydreams mixed with a smattering of lust.

Cakes and weddings.

"So, is that a yes?" she asked, her mind firmly fixed on the business at hand.

"Yes. But you're going to be the one owing me when this is all said and done."

"Fine." She waved Seth away from the bar and closer to the table. And tapped on a glass with her knife. "May I have your attention?"

The room quieted. "It's time to cut the cake. Tom and Susan, would you do the honors?"

The bride and groom took up their position in front of the elaborate, five tiered cake. No Leaning Tower of Pisa today, no Barbie cake topper, and best of all, no impression of Seth's butt in the center of it.

No, this was a beautiful, traditional, un-sat-in cake. The photographer snapped pictures as Tom and Susan ran their knife through the sweet confection.

The happy couple cut two slices and placed them on a napkin then handed them to Desi, who in turn handed one to Seth.

She smiled and faced the crowd gathered around them. "I know that a modern-day tradition is that the bride and groom would now feed each other a piece of cake. And somewhere along the line, that sweet tradition turned into a smash-fest. But since the bride looks so lovely, we're not going to mess with perfection. My assistant, Seth, and I will play stand-ins for the cake smashing."

The audience clapped loudly.

Desi offered a slice to Seth. "Seth?"

They intertwined their arms and held the cake in front of each other's mouth.

And for a moment, Desi looked into Seth's deep blue eyes and she could almost believe that it was for real...that this was the man she loved and she had just promised to spend the rest of her life with him.

Desi smashed her piece into his face, hoping to break whatever spell he'd cast on her.

Seth grinned through the icing as he pushed his slice into her face with a twist.

"Kiss, kiss, kiss," the guests all chanted.

Desi knew that they were talking about the bride and groom, heard their collective exhale and cheering as the happy couple obliged them and kissed, but she barely noticed it. What she did notice was how cute Seth was with icing all over his face, and he seemed to be coming closer, closer, closer, as if he was going to kiss her as well.

Only he didn't.

No, Seth, took his napkin and wiped part of the icing off her face.

Desi tried to hide her disappointment as she tore the veil from her head and said, "Let's leave the happy couple and go get cleaned up."

Noting that the catering staff had started cutting and serving the cake and that everything else was in order, she led him into the kitchen. She kept wiping at the cake as they walked into the back office where she'd set up her command central for this reception.

She tossed the veil on the desk and turned to her assistant.

"For someone who didn't want to do it, you certainly have a way with smashing cakes."

He was wiping at his cake-covered face.

"Here let me help," she said, moving toward him.

He took a step backwards. "I can do it."

"But you've missed some frosting right here." She wiped a bit of frosting from next to his left eye.

"And right here," she said, moving down and towards his nose. "There. Did I get it all off me?"

"Not quite."

"Could you help me?" He took a napkin and slowly, gently dabbed at her face.

He moved closer, studying her. "Did you know your face is asymmetrical?"

"Pardon?"

"It's not quite the same on both sides. Your right eye is just a little larger than your left and …"

The napkin stilled on her face, as Seth stopped speaking. "And?" she prompted.

"And looking at you makes me want to kiss you."

He was echoing her own thoughts and rather than make her happy, it made her nervous.

She should simply walk away and forget about him. After all, Seth Rutherford was on the rebound. He wasn't her type. She wanted a prince charming. No, he wasn't her type at all. As a matter of fact, he was her parent's type. He—

He had a cat named Schrodinger, which meant he had a quiet sense of humor.

He forgave his runaway bride, which meant he had a kind and generous heart.

She couldn't wrestle out the why's and not's of kissing Seth, so she simply said, "So why don't you?"

He didn't kiss her, instead, he studied her, looking perplexed as he said, "I hardly know you. I can't stop thinking about you, about touching you. That doesn't mean I should kiss you."

"It doesn't mean you shouldn't."

"But…" Whatever he was going to say was lost as his lips touched hers. Or did her lips touch his?

She wasn't sure, but it didn't matter. What mattered was that their lips were touching. There was no gentle introduction here, just raw, hot need.

Desi was overwhelmed by the taste, the scent, the feel of him. Frosting on his lips. Sweet and strong. An underlying scent of the outdoors, wild and fresh. And the feel…she took a step closer, melding her body to his. There was so much warmth in his embrace and she wanted more of it.

"Seth," she said, pulling back. "I was wrong, we shouldn't do this."

"What was that?" He stepped back and stared at her.

"Pardon?"

"You kissed me," he said, an accusation in his voice.

"No," she corrected him. "You kissed me."

"Why?"

"I don't know. Why did you kiss me?"

He shook his head and took another step backwards. "I don't know and I don't like it."

"You didn't like my kiss?" Granted, it had been a while since she kissed anyone, but Desi thought she hadn't lost all her skills.

"No, I mean yes. I liked your kiss, but I don't know why I liked it. When I kissed Mary Kathryn it was nice, but... well, this was different than that and I'm not sure why. As a scientist I need to know why. I mean, you've got great assets—I might have been drunk, but I notice when you put me into your car. And I've dreamed about them every night this week. But they're just physical. Physical attraction is... well, it's a chemical, hormonal thing. It's nothing to base a relationship on."

"Who's talking about relationships?" she asked. She needed to remind both of them that this kiss couldn't lead anywhere.

"But I kissed you," he said.

Trying to adopt a cavalier attitude, Desi said, "Seth, this is the twenty-first century. Kissing me doesn't compromise my virtue. I'm not waiting for a proposal of marriage based on it."

"Good, because I'm not getting married. Ever. There are just too many variables involved. I could never be sure of it. But I'd like to compromise your virtue. And that's what's got me so confused. I was friends with Mary Kathryn for years, worked with her every day and I never once wanted to strip her naked in an office."

"And that's what we need to remember. We're in the office, and there's a wedding out in the hall. A wedding I'm responsible for. You made me forget about it. And though my parents might not think being a wedding coordinator is a lofty career, it's mine and it's important. I don't forget about it."

Seth didn't say a word. He was staring at her in a rather befuddled fashion.

"Listen, it was just a kiss. Forget it. I'm going to. Let's get back there and see to it this reception goes without a hitch."

Forget about it?

Seth wished he could forget about that darned kiss yesterday. But he couldn't seem to. He'd spent the night definitely not forgetting it.

He remembered every detail of yesterday's wedding in vivid detail. He was relieved he'd done better than the first wedding, that he hadn't destroyed anything or anyone. No, it wasn't the wedding that bothered him, but his reaction to Desi.

Even though he analyzed it, he couldn't figure out what was going on between him and Desi. He'd never felt such primal responses to a woman. If it was just that elemental reaction, he could ignore it. But there was something more going on. He genuinely liked her. He'd showed up early at her apartment yesterday, not because he was always early— he wasn't—but because he couldn't wait another minute to see her again.

"Darn, Schrodinger, what am I going to do?"

"Merp."

"Yeah, that about sums it up. Merp."

He'd watched Desi handle the rest of the reception yesterday with grace and a deftness. She seemed to be everywhere at once.

Everywhere but where he was.

She'd kept her distance after they'd smashed the cake and kissed, almost as if he made her nervous.

But that couldn't be. From what he could see, Desdemona Smith was fearless.

She ignored her parents wishes and chased after her dream. He wasn't sure when she'd started *Engaging Styles*, but from what he could see, she was a success with it. She managed drunken grooms, runaway brides, smashed cakes, and even terminal hiccups with grace and style.

She was fearless and good at what she did... and she was avoiding him. When he'd said goodbye, she'd simply given him an absent-minded wave and *thank you*, but never truly looked at him.

He wanted to talk to her, to discuss their kiss with her. Maybe she'd have some additional data that would allow him to form a hypothesis, but she obviously was keeping her distance. He couldn't come up with a theory without all the data and he couldn't get all the data he needed without Desi's help.

It was obvious she wasn't interested in helping him analyze their almost chemical reaction to each other. She was avoiding him.

But he had an ace up his sleeve.

"Hello, Desi. Remember that tit-for-tat thing you talked about... well, you had your tits, now it's time for my tat..."

CHAPTER SIX

Sunday mornings were meant for lounging in bed reading the paper. They were meant for brunches and lazing about. They weren't meant for taking life in hand and hitting the open sea—lake.

She'd promised herself she'd forget Seth Rutherford after the wedding, but then he'd called talking about tits for tats and since she owed him, she had to put off her forgetting for one more day.

Desi gulped convulsively, not sure she'd ever manage to forget this trip. She'd be okay if the darned boat stopped rocking so fiercely. Lake Erie seemed bigger from a boat in the water than it did from on shore.

"What kind of assistant has a freak bathtub accident?" she asked between gulps.

Bigger and rougher. Despite the bright afternoon sun, there was a brisk wind kicking up waves. And Seth's boat, *The Guppy*, didn't look big enough to withstand too many waves. It wasn't much more than a rowboat with a motor on it. Oh, there were several seats near the steering wheel and a couple more at the side facing the water. There was some flat deck space, but Desi suspected the boat would be more at home in a tub than on the great lake.

She was sitting next to Seth, who was driving. A debt was a debt—but really this was going to heck with the deal.

"And who names their boat *The Guppy* anyway?" She fought back another wave of nausea that crashed against her fragile stomach like the big waves crashed against the boat's hull.

"My assistant fell in the tub and broke his ankle and as for naming my boat *The Guppy*. It's a joke. You see, when Tony and I were about eleven, we went to swimming lessons together and he was miffed because I was put in the dolphin class and he was back in the guppies."

"Seth?" Desi said, seeing a flash of pain on his face as he finished the swimming story.

"Mary Kathryn's with him. We talked and she said that neither of them wanted to hurt me. I'm not sure about much, but I am sure about that. She sounded … well, happy. I loved Mary Kathryn. Still do. But I've spent the last week thinking about us and about what went wrong and I've realized I was never *in love* with her. I don't really know if I'm capable of something that…" he paused, as if he was searching for the correct scientific term.

"Emotional," Desi supplied.

"Yeah, maybe. It seems to me that phrases like *in love* are bandied around all the time, but judging from the number of divorces, it seems a rather fickle emotion. Tenuous. More of a chemical reaction that dissipates rapidly than any lasting relationship."

"You told me before you weren't in love with Mary Kathryn."

"Kate," he said.

Desi could hear the confusion in his voice.

"She says Tony calls her Kate. She says she always dreamed of being a Kate. I never knew that. To me she was always Mary Kathryn. She's staying in Houston with him where she'll be a Kate full-time. He runs an Irish Pub and

Sushi Bar. She said on the phone that he was going to have to cook his sushi because of the contaminants. He was in the background yelling that his sushi isn't contaminated."

"Ah, see, they're already fighting." Desi felt almost gleeful. She'd like to smash Tony "*The Guppy*" Donetti for hurting Seth.

Seth might be behaving nobly about this whole best friend running away with his fiancée thing, but Desi didn't feel noble at all. She was outraged on Seth's behalf.

He might deny it, might rattle on about not feeling deep emotions, but he must be hurt and confused. She'd do just about anything to fix that.

Why? Why did it matter to her?

Maybe it was a feeling of debt. Maybe it was simply that she liked him. She thought about... thought about his defending her to her parents, about his pitching in and helping, though it was obvious working at weddings wasn't his forte. She even thought about his cat and its silly name.

She liked him and she didn't want to see him hurt.

"No, it wasn't a fight. She started laughing as he hollered. I mean, I've heard her laugh before—once we read this article about Prigogine's theory of self-organization and Mary Kathryn said I could have been his case-study and we both laughed about that—but we never laughed like she and Tony were. It was... well, maybe sensual is a good word. And he was in the background laughing as well. Mary Kathryn, Kate, and I worked together for over a year but never had anything like that. Not that intimate."

He sat a moment, looking as if he was trying to digest the thought of Mary Kathryn, his research partner, turning into a sensually laughing Kate.

"Let's face it—the only heat between us was our Bunsen burner. I'm happy she's found someone," he finally said.

"I'm happy for her and Tony. I love them both and hope they're happy."

"You're a good man, Seth Rutherford," she said.

She was struck by the accuracy of that statement. Desi might not know many things, but she knew in every fiber of her being that Seth was a truly good man.

"No. I'm a simple man. I found out just in time that things would never have been simple with Mary Kathryn."

Simply wonderful.

That's how she'd describe Seth at this moment.

He might deny his ability to feel deeply, yet she knew that he meant what he'd just said. He willingly forgave Tony and Kate. He loved them both enough to be happy for their happiness.

Yeah, he was simply wonderful.

"Okay, enough of that. Let's get to work and see what we have."

Desi followed Seth's directions. There was a snake-like tube on the deck of the boat. She helped Seth lift and place it in the water. He used the tube to collect his samples of the lake's sediment and as he did, examine the contents from the bottom of the lake. In amongst the sand were rocks and all sorts of creepy crawly shelled things.

Desi hated things that crept.

Smooshy, yucky looking things.

They gave her little shivers down her spine.

She'd almost flunked biology in high school because she refused to dissect a worm.

"What a haul. Why, look at that beauty," Seth murmured as he stared at the sample. A pinky-nail sized gross thing lay in the center of his palm.

"Zebra mussels aren't native to the Great Lakes. They appeared in the mid-eighties. They've been a mixed blessing. They've helped clean the lake, and yet, they've thrown the entire ecosystem out of whack," he said, slipping into his teacher mode seemingly without any effort. "They stick together and clog up water intake systems and—"

He looked up and stared at her. "Are you okay?"

"No." Desi was desperately trying to keep from screaming like a girl. That creature in Seth's hand gave her the willies. "What's the matter?"

"I'm just a little seasick, that's all." Seasick sounded better than scared of a glorified slug.

"Oh, well, try to focus on something else. Here. Look at this beauty." He dumped the zebra mussel into her hand.

Seth was prepared for Desi to ooh and ah.

He was prepared for her to study the specimen.

He wasn't prepared for her shriek or for the mussel to go flying across the boat. And he especially wasn't prepared to have it land right between his eyes with a nice little *thwack*.

But Desi obviously wasn't prepared either...wasn't set for the fact that *The Guppy* was a small boat. As she backed up, wiping her hand on her shorts as if she was trying to wipe childhood cooties off her hand, she'd backed right over the side into the churning lake waters.

Seth's heart squeezed into his throat.

"Desi!" he screamed as he raced to the edge.

He saw her safe within her orange life vest, bobbing next to the boat.

"Here, grab my hand." He leaned over the edge and thrust his hand toward her.

She smiled then and reached up.

He pulled.

Desi braced her feet against the side of the boat, but rather than pulling herself up as he expected—as any sane, rational person would do—she pulled him down.

Hard.

Seth went toppling over the side, head first into the water as well. He immediately bobbed up to the surface because of his life vest.

"What did you do that for?" he burbled as he choked on the water he'd inhaled on the way down.

"I don't know," she said, laughing.

Laughing hard.

There was something familiar in that laugh. Seth bobbed in the lake, desperately trying to analyze what it was as he studied her.

Then it hit him.

Desi's laugh had the same quality to it as Mary Kathryn's had when she was on the phone laughing with Tony. Sensual.

It made him think about the kiss they'd shared.

Looking for a diversion, he did the only thing he could think of. He swam for the still laughing Desi and said, "That wasn't nice," just before he dunked her.

She bobbed, in a life-vested induced way, like an apple in a barrel. She came up still laughing as she coughed and sputtered. At that moment, Seth did something totally out of character.

He laughed.

Not a small chuckle or a quiet laugh he might make politely at any faculty party when someone made a joke.

No, this was a laugh ripped from the tips of his toes that traveled throughout his body, gaining momentum, until the moment it burst forth and rang out.

It surprised him.

Maybe it surprised Desi too, because she stopped sputtering and laughing, and simply stared at him a moment. She looked at him as if he was something rather foreign and mystifying.

Then, just as suddenly, she was laughing again. "You think you can take me on and win? Well, you asked for it, Rutherford."

"Oh, yeah?"

"Yeah. Prepare to be conquered."

Conquered. That's just how he felt as he spent the next half an hour playing in the water. Conquered by a brunette with green eyes and a quick smile. The thought was more alien than his laughter.

To be conquered by a small laughing woman who reminded him that there was more to Lake Erie's water than zebra mussels and gobies, it was…

For once in his life, he refused to over-analyze the situation.

Seth pushed all worries about Desi's affect on him and instead just allowed himself to relax. They played freely, carelessly. Like overgrown children who didn't have a worry in the world.

There were no runaway brides, no worries about careers.

There was the sun and the waves…

And there was Seth and Desi.

For that moment in time, it just simply was.

And the fact that it *was* enough for Seth.

"I think I'm as pruned as an eighty-year-old woman." Desi had just dunked him for the umpteenth time and held up her hand and examined the wrinkled skin.

"Are you ready to get back in the boat?" he asked. He kept his tone light, though the question was tinged with regret.

It was almost as if Lake Erie had mystically made him forget himself. As soon as he left its dark waters, he knew that the magic would fade. And rather than see the world as magic, he'd once again fade into a logical view.

"Don't make it sound as if us being out here is my fault. You're the one who dunked me," Desi said. "It's your fault I'm all wrinkled."

"You're the one who pulled me into the water," Seth teased back.

"Well, only after you put that slimy thing in my hand."

"It's not a slimy thing. It's a zebra mussel. I've been studying their effects on the lake for the last two years."

"It doesn't matter what you call it, its still slimy."

Seth knew whose fault it was that he'd just spent part of his afternoon playing instead of working and he'd have to think of some way to thank her for that. "Come on. Let's get out of here. You first."

The small ladder at the side made getting out of the water easier, but the life vests were bulky, and so it took Desi a few extra minutes to climb up. And Seth spent those extra minutes studying her form. Well, studying all of her form that was visible to him. Her short-covered bottom.

He realized that a cold lake wasn't enough to chill the heat that raced through his body as he stared at Desi.

She made it onto the boat and put an end to his agony.

No, actually, she made it worse. As he reached the top of the ladder, he realized she'd stripped off her life vest, shorts and t-shirt. She was clad only in a demure tank bathing suit that looked anything but demure. It hugged her body in all the right places as she toweled herself off.

"Gosh, the lake is colder than I thought. I'm freezing."

Seth stared at the samples on the deck of the boat.

"Here," she said, a towel hit him across the chest. "You'd better dry off, too."

"I'm fine."

He gulped as she sat on the deck of the boat and turned her face toward the sun. She looked like some Greek Goddess.

Like Eve.

Only instead of offering him an apple, she was his apple and he wanted nothing more than to take a bite.

Seth shook his head.

What was with him today? He'd just recently been with a woman who had everything in common with him, a woman who should have been perfect, but wasn't.

How could he be thinking about Desi like this?

"Seth, what on earth is the matter with you? Are you waterlogged or what?"

"I'm—" he stopped, unable to say another word.

"Sit down before you fall down. I know you're all work, but if this is how playing in the water for a little while affects you, you obviously have a problem."

She reached up, took his hand, and pulled him onto the deck next to her. "Now dry off and warm up."

"I think I'm warm enough."

"You can't be. That water was chilly."

"No. No, I'm not chilly."

She reached over and took his hand. "Hey, you're not."

Seth pulled it back, as if her touch burned.

"What's wrong? Are you mad at me because I pulled you into the water? Really, I was just teasing. I thought you had fun."

"No, I'm not mad. And I did have fun."

"So, what's eating you?"

"You." The word was out before he could stop it.

She was obviously as surprised by his statement as he was to have made it.

"Pardon?" she asked.

"You're not really eating me, I'm simply fantasizing about you."

"Pardon?" she repeated.

"You sound so prim and proper when you say *pardon*" he mimicked her inflection, "like that, but I don't think you really are. I think..." he paused, studying her.

Before he could change his mind, he leaned toward her, forgetting everything but the desire to kiss her. And though there was no frosting on them this time, she was still sweet.

Intoxicating.

Addictive.

Seth heard someone groan. Maybe it was him.

He was groaning over Desi?

The thought sobered him and he broke off the kiss.

She reached up and touched her lips, as if their kiss had somehow left a mark. "What did you do that for?"

"I'm not sure." Seth hadn't known what he was doing since the day of his almost-wedding. But maybe it wasn't the almost wedding that had confused things. Maybe it was Desi?

"But maybe I want to do it again?" he added.

"Are you asking me or telling me?" she asked.

"Telling you. But—" What on earth was he saying?

"Desi, I'm as confused by this as you are. Probably more so. Let's finish up here, then, if you'd like, I want you to come home with me."

"Pardon?" she asked for a third time.

Desi was sure she'd heard Seth wrong. She must still have water in her ears from her impromptu trip overboard. She wiggled her index fingers around in them, hoping to clear her hearing before he repeated himself.

"Come home with me," Seth repeated. "I'll make you dinner."

She tried to keep her face neutral, tried not to let him see the way her heart lightened just a bit at his suggestion.

"Are you a good cook?" she asked instead of saying, *yes, Seth. I'd love to go home with you.*

"Yes," he said, in that serious way of his, as if her question was one of earth shattering importance, rather than a just a joke. "I'm a very good cook. I know how to make a meal that optimizes nutritional values and minimizes calories."

"Uh, Seth are you implying I'm fat?" she teased him, hoping to throw him as off balanced as she felt.

"No. You're not fat."

"It sounded as if you were suggesting I might be." At the serious look on his face, she realized that Seth wasn't used to being teased.

He tried again. "No, you're not fat. I like how you look. I mean, I *really* like how you look. I can't stop thinking about how you look. In fact, I've dreamed about it. And—"

"Burgers," she said, interrupting him.

She wasn't sure if she was pleased he found her attractive and had been thinking about her or just nervous. She was sure that she needed a safer subject.

"What?" he asked.

"Burgers. Hamburgers. After a day on the lake, I don't want to maximize nutrition and minimize calories. I want burgers. Big, greasy ones with French fries."

"Do you know what a meal like that does to your cholesterol levels?" he asked.

"Yep. But sometimes you just have to throw caution to the wind and live on the wild side. Sometimes it's okay to have fun, Seth." She paused, watching him take her comment in and grinned as she added, "And milkshakes. I like strawberry best. How 'bout you?"

She was ready for more arguments on the health risks associated with fast food, but all he said was, "Chocolate. Rich, thick chocolate."

"Let's go then. I'm hungry."

They changed into dry clothes in the public restrooms after they'd docked *The Guppy*. Desi was glad she had an extra outfit in a bag.

She followed him to the parking lot. Watching him walk. For the first time she noticed that he had an amazingly tight butt for a professor. Actually, for anyone.

Not that it should matter. Seth wasn't her type. He was her parents' type, and that made him as far from her type as you could humanly get. She was just being nice. Friendly.

They drove from the dock, up State Street, the top of Seth's convertible down, the wind blowing through her hair and her mind running in circles.

Yeah, friendly.

Of course, she'd forgotten she'd promised herself to forget Seth Rutherford when she said she'd eat with him. Well, she'd forget about him after dinner.

Desi was just having dinner with Seth because he was good company. It had nothing to do with the toe-tingling experience of kissing him, not once, but twice. It had nothing to do with the assets she'd been admiring. It didn't even have anything to do with the fact that he was extremely cute when he got all serious and enthusiastic about tiny little slimy slugs.

Nope, not at all.

Desdemona Smith was simply an altruistic, generous human being. That's all.

Ordering burgers at a drive-through window interrupted her inner musings, but soon with grease ladened burgers in hand she was thinking again.

Seth was a nice guy. But Desi wanted more than nice.

She wanted someone who was madly in love with her.

Someone who couldn't live without her. A passionate, adventurous soul mate.

Someone who would sweep her off her feet and carry her away to a happily-ever after.

Look at how quickly Seth had recovered from losing Mary Kathryn. That definitely isn't a sign of a deeply, passionate sort of man. Add to that, the only carrying away had been when she carried his drunken self up his front stairs.

Of course, he'd defended her to her parents.

That was hero-ish.

But...

She realized the car had stopped and Seth had opened her door for her. "Here we are."

Desi followed him into his house, no closer to sorting out her feelings than when she'd started thinking. She pushed her worries away and took in Seth's place now that she could see it plainly.

It was every bit as organized as she'd imagined a little over a week ago in the murky light. And she'd been right— the walls were white. Dull, institutional white.

Something brushed against her leg. "Hey, Schrodinger."

Desi knelt down and stroked the shabby cat's fur. "How you doing, Dingie."

"Dingie?" Seth asked, pausing as he carried the food into the kitchen.

"Well, Schrodinger is a bit of a mouthful, don't you think?"

"I named him after—"

"Erwin Schrodinger. A physicist with a theory about a cat in a box being alive and dead at the same time. It's sort of like the question, if a tree falls in the woods and no one is around, does it still make a noise?"

"How did you know that?" he asked, looking confused. He pulled two plates out of the cupboard and loaded their artery-clogging goodies onto them.

Desi took her plate and milkshake over to the small table in the corner. "You mean, how would a wedding coordinator know about a twentieth century physicist?"

Seth sat next to her. "I didn't mean to—"

"Of course you did. But despite the fact that I'm a *mere wedding coordinator* doesn't mean I don't know things."

She bit into her burger. "Oh, this is heavenly. Try yours."

She swallowed, then said, "Back to Schrodinger. There are subjects I'm not well versed in, but science...Well, my parents wanted to turn me into a Nobel Prize winning scientist. I mean, instead of summer camp, you know the kind where you ride horses and swim? I went to science camp. It wasn't bad, but it wasn't what I wanted."

"Parents should respect a child's interests," Seth said, solemnly, then took a bite.

"How about yours?" she asked.

"How about mine, what?"

"Your parents. Did they respect your interest in science?"

"They never really cared. No, that's not quite right. They love me, I know that, and they cared—care. It's just that they were always so wrapped up in each other and their private dramas that I just faded into the background and they never really noticed me."

"I'm sorry," Desi said softly.

"Sorry for what?"

"You deserve to be noticed." In her mind's eye she saw Seth at the reception, standing alone, quietly watching the people.

"I prefer not to be. Really. It was better that they left me alone. They were always so…volatile. I wasn't. I never want that type of relationship. On again, off again. Loud fights, louder reconciliations. That's why I want order. Some sense. I—" He stopped short and then mumbled, "Never mind."

"Listen, let's finish these burgers before they get cold," she said with forced cheerfulness.

She wished Seth wouldn't have stopped.

She suddenly remembered the science fair again. She'd watched as Seth got up to accept his award. Her secret girl-hood crush and she'd found a way to help him. Her ecstatic feeling had threatened to overwhelm her.

He'd looked so good up there on the stage, waiting to accept his award, she could see his pleasure hidden beneath his serious exterior.

She thought of the man he'd grown into. Maybe his parents' relationship explained a lot about Seth's willingness to marry someone because she was comfortable.

Desi looked across the table and noticed a small drop of the burger's special sauce on his chin. Without thinking, she reached across the table and wiped it off.

Seth moved back, as if she'd pinched him. "What are you doing?"

Desi let her hand fall back onto her lap. "You had sauce dripping down your chin."

Seth took a napkin.

"I got it all," she assured him.

"You got it all off me maybe, but your sandwich was apparently as drippy as mine."

She reached for a napkin and wiped at her own face, but Seth stopped her. "Allow me."

He reached over and wiped her face for her. It felt more like a caress. Like when he'd wiped the cake from her face at the wedding yesterday.

"Seth." That's all she could think to say, just his name. He'd confessed he'd thought about her. And right at this minute, she wanted to shout out her own confession as well—that she couldn't get him out of her mind—but she couldn't make the words come out.

Wouldn't let them.

He sat back in his seat. "Maybe we should talk about this."

"*This?*" she asked, her voice little more than a squeak.

"This. Whatever this attraction is that's between us. In my experience—"

"Seth, I don't want to talk about it. I don't want to analyze it. I just want to—"

She didn't know she was going to do it, until she did it. She leaned toward him and let herself go. His lips felt as if they were frozen, as if they were shocked by her forwardness, but then there was some kind of release, as if something had been released and he began kissing her back. More than that, he took over.

Hunger.

That's what he felt like. A man who was hungry for what she could give him. The feeling was powerful. Desi was almost high with it.

He pulled her from her chair onto his lap. As his hand threaded through her hair, he groaned.

"I still think we should talk about this. I can't seem to keep my hands off you."

He might be analyzing again, but Desi was pleased to note he hadn't released her. He wrapped her in his arms. She liked the way she felt, safe in his embrace.

"Listen, Seth, I think it's obvious that there's something between us and since we're both consenting adults, there's no reason we can't..." she let the sentence trail off, suddenly not sure what to say.

"I don't know why this keeps happening. I keep trying to figure it out, but end up simply chasing my thoughts in circles. We don't have anything in common."

He looked so cute when he was confused. Desi didn't think he'd appreciate hearing it. "It's not as if that hasn't occurred to me as well. I want romance. I want the prince on his charger carrying me off to his castle—the whole package."

"And I'm not romantic," he said. "I don't know how to be. I want logic and order. And this isn't—"

"Maybe we could bypass the romance and forget about logic and—"

"But we should discuss this and weigh all the factors." There was a small furrow in his brow, as if scrinching up his forehead would help him figure out the complexities of their mutual cases of lust.

Desi reached up and gently ran a finger through the furrow. "Seth, I have a confession, I don't want to worry about our differences. I think we've proved we have one overwhelmingly big similarity. I want you so bad it hurts. I want all of you, now."

CHAPTER SEVEN

It was as if Desi's confession freed something in Seth. "Me, too. I want you that bad."

"Then what are we waiting for?"

"I can't promise the things you said you wanted, but I promise I'll try." He promptly tried to scoop her into his arms. "You're an awkward shape, you know."

"Oh, no. You're not going to start figuring out if I'm a rectangular solid or a sphere, are you?" She wasn't sure he remembered that particular conversation in the car, but she did.

"I don't need to calculate mass, in this case. I just need to find a better means of levering you up."

"Seth, I can walk. You're going to hurt something if you carry me."

"You wanted romance and though I'm no Cyrano, I know carrying a woman into your room to make love is romantic."

"Not if you're going to break your back," she pointed out. "I can walk."

"Okay, so maybe cradling you and standing isn't going to work. We'll adapt."

"Adapt?" she asked, not sure she liked the sounds of that.

"Yeah." He stood up as well, and studied her, a crooked grin on his face. "I think I've got it."

Without waiting for her to say anything, he bent and threw her body over his shoulder into a fireman's hold.

"Seth, I don't think this is what the romance novels mean when they say he carried her into his bedroom."

"Ah, but as a scientist I've learned that there are frequently a multitude of solutions to any one problem."

She was laughing as she thumped at his back and she was pretty sure he was as well, judging from the small shake of his shoulders. "Put me down."

"No, I'm carrying you into my room and then … what's the proper romantic word?"

Making love. That's the phrase she wanted to blurt out, but instead, she kept her tone light and said, "Ravish. You're going to ravish me."

"Ravish. Oh, that sounds as if it has potential." He paused mid-stairs. "Dingie, get out of the way."

"Don't you drop me," Desi cried, unable to see where they were going. No, what she could see was a whole new perspective on Seth's behind. Even from that angle, it was a fine looking backside.

Despite the fact they were laughing, her desire was as hot and heavy as before. Maybe even hotter.

She wanted this man. Wanted him more than anything.

She wanted to laugh with him. Wanted to tease him. She wanted to keep the world from hurting him.

She just wanted him.

They reached the top of the stairs, and Seth turned to the left. "Here we are."

Desi was suddenly flipped back over his shoulder onto his bed. "Do you feel romanced?"

There was a smile on his face that said he was joking, the sight caused her heart to constrict.

Seth Rutherford was about to make love to her, to ravish her, and he was joking.

Emotions that Desi was hard-pressed to identify seemed to squeeze all the oxygen from her body.

"Yes, that was plenty romantic enough," she said, trying to keep her tone light.

"Good, because I don't think I could have thought of much more to do than this…"

Desi woke before Seth the next morning. As far as she was concerned, this was the way to start a Monday. She was acutely aware of the heat of his body pressed against her nakedness. Skin to skin. They lay entwined, mingling until it was hard to know where Desi left off and Seth started.

She knew her hair must be a fright. Pieces were plastered across the front of her neck. And she didn't even want to think about her breath. Morning breath was a given.

But instead of worrying, Desi chose to watch Seth. Asleep, his serious expression relaxed. A lock of his beach-blond hair lay across his forehead. She would have liked to move it, to push it back into place, but she didn't want to wake him. So she just lay there, contentedly watching him.

Content.

That's how she felt here, with Seth. Content. Satiated. Happy. Painfully, blissfully happy.

Gradually, he stirred, waking slowly, and she sensed when he became aware that he wasn't alone.

His eyes bolted open and he stared at her.

"*Umm*," was all he said.

It was a nervous sort of sound that people make when they want to fill up the quiet space, but couldn't really think of anything worthwhile to fill it with.

"Now, that's just what a woman wants to hear after she's spent a night with a man. *Umm*. Of course, when it's accompanied by that worried look you're currently wearing, it's even more flattering. Are you *umming* me because you're not sure what to do with me? Were you hoping I'd left, so you didn't have to deal with the messy morning-after-itis? Or did I maybe misinterpret your tone and was that a more sexual sort of *umm?*"

Teasing obviously wasn't going to help ease the tension. He looked so unbelievably flustered and uncomfortable that Desi put aside her own worries of bedhead and morning breath and tried to think of something to do.

Before she could come up with a plan he said, "Desi, I'm not sure what happened. I mean …"

"Seth," she said gently, "I'm sure with all those science classes you took and have taught, you had at least a smattering of biology."

There, she'd done it. He smiled, and some of the worry dissipated.

"Yes. I think I understand that part." He chuckled. A rich, low, rumbling sound that reverberated throughout Desi's system.

"It's the rest," he said. "I mean, I told you Mary Kathryn and I never … I knew her for a long time and was planning to marry her. Yet, she never made me feel the kind of desperation I felt with you last night. Last night, I needed you so much."

She was going to ignore the fact that he'd just brought up his ex-fiancée and concentrate on the fact he'd used the word desperation.

Desperation. That sounded good.

He was desperate for her? Oh, yeah, she liked the sound of that. She'd felt a bit of desperation herself last night. But unlike Seth, didn't feel the need to analyze it this morning.

"And how about this morning?" she asked. "Any aches and pains you want to talk about?"

"I just didn't want you to think I'd used you to satisfy some hormone-based lust. It was more than that. It was..."

He left the sentence hang a half beat too long.

Desi knew he didn't have a clue what it was, and she wasn't insulted, because neither did she. She could list all the reasons why things with Seth would never workout long term. He was on the rebound, they had nothing in common—except maybe this. She reached out and touched his chest.

No, she wasn't about to spend the day trying to figure out whatever this was with him. She didn't want to quantify it or label it. She had other plans.

"Seth, in those biology classes did anyone ever mention that females are known to experience a bit of lust too? Because, if not, let me guarantee you that they do and I did. I still do. So if there was *using* going on, it was both of us. A little mutual lust is a good thing, nothing to look so worried about. And if you're willing, I was thinking that last night wasn't enough...I'm not quite as satisfied as I thought. Maybe you'd consider doing some mutual lusting this morning?"

Suddenly all worry and confusion disappeared. In its place was a good dose of the lust they'd been discussing.

"Not quite satisfied?" Seth asked. "Well, we can't have that, can we? I think I'm up for the job."

"Hold that thought and give me two minutes," Desi said. She might not be able to do much about the bedhead, but she refused to make love to Seth until she'd brushed her teeth.

She scampered out of bed and into his bathroom. She didn't have a toothbrush, but rubbed his toothpaste around in her mouth with her index finger and tried to smooth down the worst of her hair.

He took a turn in the bathroom when she finished.

She was still trying to de-mess her hair when he came back and climbed into bed.

"You don't have to do that," he said.

"Do what?"

"Primp for me." He pulled her into his arms. "Because, I have a confession."

She snuggled closer. "Oh, do tell. I love knowing your deep, dark secrets."

"This one's not so deep and dark. You look lovely."

Desi laughed. "I think you may need glasses, Seth."

"Oh, no." He traced the bridge of her nose with his finger, just a light, casual touch, but it was enough to make her heart rate accelerate. "Would you like a detailed account of your loveliness?"

"Pardon?"

"There you go, being all prim and proper again. I love when you say *pardon* like that."

He ran his fingers through her hair, taking a section and letting it fall, strand by strand. "And I love the way your hair isn't really just brown. Look. There's light blonde and even a few reddish streaks in this. Variegated. That's a good word for your hair. I love looking at it. Yesterday on the lake, when the sun hit it, I was mesmerized. And this morning, it's even more captivating."

His fingers still threaded in her hair, he continued, "And your eyes. They remind me of the lake. Sometimes they're greyish and sometimes, like right now, they're a greenish grey. Sometimes there's even a touch of blue green."

"Contacts. I wear those extended-wear contacts."

"Sh. I'm working on collecting scientific data. Now, where was I? Oh, your chin."

She touched her chin, but didn't feel anything exceptional about it. "My chin?"

"Oh, yeah. I like your chin. It's absolutely lovely. It's got the smallest little line in it."

"A cleft." She'd never noticed a cleft in her chin.

"No, not really. Just a little line, a crease maybe is a better word. When you smile, it's noticeable and I love seeing it."

She'd never had anyone talk to her like this and felt a little flustered with it.

"Well, thank you," she said to mask her feelings. "I think you're learning this waxing poetic stuff at an accelerated rate. Want to hear what I like about you?"

"No, it's still my turn," he said and shook his hair. A small section spilled across his forehead. "You see, there's more."

Desi brushed his hair back and realized what he'd said. "More?"

"Well, I have to confess, there's a lot more. Let's see, I was on your chin. You know how I like to be orderly about things. We'll just work sequentially our way down my list of things I like."

He dropped her hair and gently caressed her neck. "I like your neck. It's long, and elegant looking. Like a swan. And below your neck..."

He wiggled his eyebrows and grinned.

A playful Seth was a sight to behold. Desi was enjoying every second. "Do tell, Mr. Rutherford."

"Well, they're a nicely matched pair."

So saying, he leaned down and focused every bit of his considerable concentration on her breasts.

"Seth," she said, her voice all hazy and breathy. Desi hardly recognized the sound of it.

This wasn't some leftover girlhood infatuation. It wasn't simply a hormonal attraction.

What was this man doing to her?

She wasn't sure, but Desi was happy to let him do it some more.

She was going to try to capture and memorize each moment with Seth.

But even as she did, Desi had a feeling that remembering wasn't going to be a problem at all.

Forgetting was.

CHAPTER EIGHT

"**D**id you ever imagine, all those years ago at the science fair, that we'd end up here?" Seth asked Monday afternoon.

Desi had never experienced anything like the last twenty-four hours. They'd finally left Seth's bedroom and headed downstairs to get something to eat and rather than cooking, they'd ended up on his living room floor, caught in a need that showed no signs of dimming.

"No, in high school I don't think I had enough imagination to envision something like this. Even last week, I couldn't have imagined something like this. I can't get enough of you."

Desi lay in the middle of his floor, enveloped in his arms and felt, rather than heard, his chuckle. His chest sort of quivered. She loved making him laugh.

She remembered when she'd driven him home after his almost reception. There'd been no laughter then. He'd been hurt and confused. But now, this minute, she knew that he was happy and that she'd given him that.

She wanted to give him so much more.

"Listen to that," she whispered.

"To what?"

"The rain tapping against the windows. I love the sound. It's sort of the same feeling as a good snowstorm, when the entire world's shut down and I'm safe and snug in my house, or in your house, as the case may be."

Desi had an idea. She sat up and started to pull on her clothes. "Come on."

Seth raised himself on an elbow, watching her dress. "Where are we going?"

"Out on your porch to watch the rain." She took his hand and pulled upward, though she couldn't budge him.

"Why would we want to do that? It's warm in here and dry."

"Seth, do you do anything for fun, without having a reason for it? I mean, haven't you ever just watched the rain?"

"No. What is the point?" he asked.

"There's no point, that's the point. You just stand and watch it fall, watch the sky grow darker and darker. Watch the small puddles turn into huge lakes of water. Watch the water wash down the street. You smell the rain in the air and it revitalizes you. It's clean and nourishing. And when you stand in it, you're part of something."

"Stand in it? You're not part of anything but wet," he grumbled, but he did pull his shorts back on.

"Come on, spoilsport." She pulled him out the door and onto the porch. "See, look at all that water washing down the street. You could race a boat in that stream."

"I don't have a boat here," he pointed out.

He wasn't getting her point, not getting it at all. But Desi wasn't giving up. "Okay, so you don't have a boat here. You could splash in it."

"I'd get wet."

"Seth, you're already all wet. Come on."

He shook his head. "Desi, I don't think so."

"Come on," she said, pulling him down the stairs.

Seth allowed himself to be pulled onto the sidewalk just to please Desi, not because of any dire need to be rained on.

It wasn't unpleasant. As a matter of fact the rain was warm and steady. He looked at Desi as she laughed and threw up her arms as she tilted her head backwards. "Doesn't it feel lovely?"

Lovely.

"Lovely," he murmured.

"Come on, just don't stand there." She was pulling him again, but this time Seth didn't put up any resistance. Resistance around Desi was futile. If she wanted him to play in the rain, he would. Who cared if his neighbors thought he was crazy?

He would do anything to see her smile at him, like she was right now. He'd give anything to hear the tinkle of her laughter and that included standing in an ankle deep puddle like he was right now.

"Come on, Seth, don't just stand there," and she kicked water at him.

Splashing him couldn't get him any wetter than he already was, but he knew it wasn't the wetness, but the playing she wanted. So he obliged.

"My feet are bigger and therefore have a larger surface area and can displace more water, which should mean I can make a more effective splash."

To prove the point, he kicked a huge tidal wave of a splash in her direction.

She kicked back and like a couple of kids, the battle ensued. There was no winner. But when Seth finally caught her in his arms, holding tight to restrain her from any more splashing, he knew winning didn't have a thing to do with their water battle.

He pulled her into the house without releasing her. As his lips pressed against hers and as she kissed him back, he knew he had a prize in his hands. He just wasn't sure what to do with it.

"Come on," she said. "I think I saw some canned soup in your cupboard. I'll cook for you after we dry off."

She was pulling at him again, up the stairs.

"I don't think opening a can constitutes cooking," he said, just to get a rise out of her.

"I'll have you know I'm the best canned soup cooker around. It's all in the ratio of water to soup. I don't follow the directions. I improvise."

"No, way," he said, shaking his head even as he chuckled and followed her into the bathroom. "I mean, Desi doesn't follow directions? I don't believe it. It's so out of character."

"Don't you dare mock me, Seth Rutherford. I might not follow directions, but I give them pretty good." She reached into the bathroom closet and tossed him a towel and took one for herself.

"Oh, and what are you planning to direct this evening?" he asked.

"Well, after some dry clothes—aren't we lucky that I brought extras?—and some soup, I was planning on inviting myself to sleep over again. Only I wasn't planning on a lot of sleep."

He had the towel on his head, drying his hair, and lifted the edge so he could see her. "Do tell."

"Oh, yeah. I've got tons of directions to give you tonight."

"You did tell me that you were good at that when you called me to help at the first wedding."

Seth remembered being sure then, that first wedding, that she wasn't thinking what he was thinking. And he'd been right. She wasn't. But now she was and he was right

94

about owing her, too. Oh, he owed her big time. "You also said you'd be gentle with me."

"And I was. I plan to be again tonight. Only not too gentle."

Seth couldn't sleep. He looked at the woman lying next to him. What was he doing?

Right on the heels of the thought came another—what was wrong with him? Why couldn't he take what life had so graciously tossed in his lap and simply enjoy it?

He couldn't, he realized. At least not until he'd analyzed the situation and came up with some acceptable answers. He needed to understand. He needed to think.

Quietly, he crawled out of bed and went into his office. He shut the door and turned on the light.

Here, order still reigned. His books were all nicely shelved in alphabetical order. His pencils were all sharpened, his pens neatly in their holder. His diplomas and certificates were on the wall.

There was no woman driving him crazy here. No questions he couldn't answer with a little research.

Research.

Maybe that's what he needed.

But in all his trips to the library, he couldn't ever recall seeing a book called, *There's a Woman in My Bed... Now What Do I Do?* Or even better, *There's a Woman on My Mind... How Do I Get Her Out?*

Desi had been on his mind since that first wedding. No, actually, since the rehearsal for his aborted wedding.

What was he going to do about her?

She'd single-handedly shaken his orderly world. He'd allowed her to. More than that, he'd welcomed it. Why?

Seth pulled out a piece of paper and snapped it into a clipboard.

He drew two columns. *Desi,* he wrote as a header.

What to do about Desi and this attraction?

Reasons why whatever it was between them couldn't work, he labeled one column.

He was on the rebound, just left at the altar by a woman he'd thought he'd spend the rest of his life with. A woman who shared his interests and his goals, unlike Desi. Desi was an impractical romantic. She believed in things like love at first sight, and fairytale endings. He believed in compatibility, in similar goals and interests.

He scribbled away, filling his *reasons why this infatuation can't last* side with amazing speed.

Then he thought of one thing they had going for them. *Common ground.* He wrote *Sex* under it. Then crossed it out and wrote *Good Sex.*

No. He scratched that out as well and wrote *Earth-Shattering Sex.* He put down the paper and stared at the words. No, that was wrong. What they had was more than sex, good or earth-shattering. Making love with Desi. Making love. That was what they did.

Making love with Desi was about as far removed from sex, even earth-shattering sex, as Newtonian Physics was from Quantum Mechanics.

She made him laugh. That was a plus. A huge plus. He didn't write it down, he just leaned back in his chair and let the feelings she inspired wash over him.

He couldn't remember the last time he laughed before Desi. She dragged him into the lake and out into the rain. And yet, when she was around, he felt… happy.

She made him happy.

According to this paper, they had nothing in common. Different goals. Different ideals.

Different.

He'd had everything in common with Mary Kathryn, but she'd never made him laugh, never stirred his blood. He'd never loved her. Oh, he loved her like a friend, with the same feeling of loyalty and comradery he felt for Tony. But he didn't love her deeply. And that's what made it possible for him to get over losing her with absolute pain-free ease.

No, he'd never truly loved Mary Kathryn and wished her luck with Tony. They were as odd a pairing as he was with Desi. And yet, Desi evoked such strong feelings from him. He loved her in a way that he'd never loved Mary Kathryn.

There was the physical side ... and oh, the physical side was good. But holding her after they'd made love, the feeling hadn't ebbed. That would leave him to deduct that it was more than physical. That the need he felt for Desi was something deeper, something more.

It was an emotion impossible to measure. There was no reliable quantitative data on that emotion, and yet love was the most accurate term for what he felt for Desi.

He loved her.

He'd have to tell her, but he wasn't sure how.

She was a woman who'd built a career on romance and he knew absolutely nothing about such a thing. Yet, for Desi's sake, he needed something big, something so romantic she'd forget all the logic that said they shouldn't be together and simply say she loved him, too.

CHAPTER NINE

That Wednesday, *Hazard's* was busier than usual, but Desi barely registered the overabundance of nice looking men. She was riding a wave of happiness.

Part of her wanted to tell her friends all about Seth Rutherford. But if she did they'd ask questions about what sort of relationship it was. And the truth was, Desi didn't have a clue. She refused to worry about it. Refused to worry that Seth was on the rebound, that they didn't seem to have any common ground except sex.

She refused to worry and refused to explain, so she didn't say anything to Mary Jo and Pam. She regaled them with her assistant-search woes instead.

"How hard could it be? I just need someone available Friday night and Saturdays." Before Mary Jo or Pam could answer, Desi continued, "Darn hard apparently."

Tonight she was indulging in pasta fromage, which was, despite its fancy name, nothing more than macaroni and cheese. Fancy macaroni and cheese. Millions of calories in a bowl.

She took a bite then continued. "Let's see, there was the girl with the nose ring and tattooed forehead. There have been a number of applicants who leave as soon as they find out the job requires they work on a prime-dating night. And then there was this grandfatherly type who seemed perfect until..."

Desi took another huge bite.

"Until what?" Pam asked.

"Until he told me I'd have to talk to his probation officer for him. Seems he just got out of jail."

"What'd he do?" Mary Jo asked.

"He's a flasher. He guarantees he won't do any flashing at a wedding, but can't you just see it now? The bride and groom are cutting the cake when suddenly—"

Desi stopped short, not because of worry about a flashing assistant, but because talking about cakes made her think of Seth.

Heck, breathing made her think of Seth. She couldn't get him off her mind.

"I don't think I want to see him," Pam said.

For a moment, Desi wondered if Pam read her mind and knew about her torrid affair, but then she realized that Pam was referring to the flasher.

"Me either, which is why I didn't hire him."

"So did you find anyone? If not, I can help this weekend," Pam offered, then went on, "And speaking of weekends, did I tell you about my date?"

"I may just take you up on that. And no, you didn't tell us about your date," Desi said. She took another huge bite of her calorie rich dinner as she listened to Pam's happy bubbling monologue.

"...and then he walked around and opened up the car door for me," she practically cooed.

"He didn't think you could manage it yourself?" Desi asked.

"He was just being a gentleman."

"Paul used to hold the door for me, but now I'm just happy if he'll hold a kid now and again, or maybe get a chance to hold my…" Mary Jo paused a pregnant moment and finished, "Hand now and again."

"That's not what you were going to say," Pam scolded.

"No, but it's close enough," Mary Jo said with a wicked grin.

"Look," Pam said, pointing to a lovely specimen of manhood standing across the street from the deck-side table. "Oh, that's a commando and if he asked, I'd let him hold my—"

"I thought you were dating Mr. Car-door," Desi said.

"Oh, I am, but I don't think it will last."

"Why?" Mary Jo asked. "You and Desi need to be more optimistic. Maybe he's Mr. Right."

Pam snorted. "I don't think so. Even though he's hot—and boy is he hot—and opens doors, he's not the kind of man you'd want to marry. He's got a wandering eye and wandering hands, which have momentarily wandered my way, but I don't expect them to linger long."

"So why are you seeing him?" Desi asked.

Maybe if she could figure out why Pam was in a relationship she doubted would last long, she could figure out why she was with Seth.

"Because sometimes you have to settle for Mister-Right-Now while you keep looking for Mister-Right," Pam said.

"And how will you know Mr. Right when you meet him?" Desi asked.

"I believe I just will. He'll like the same things I do, he'll want to settle down and have a family. He'll like my friends and my friends will like him. Why?"

Desi shrugged. "Just wondering."

Mister-Right-Now.

That's what Seth was. Even if they could get past their differences, he was on the rebound and would eventually bounce back into his old life—a life that didn't include her.

She was his transitional woman.

The thought didn't cheer her up. She took another sip of wine.

Seth was a man who entered relationships mind-first, not heart-first. Eventually his analytical mind would figure out how many differences stood between them.

She hoped her heart would figure it out as well.

"Oh, silk boxers," Pam yelled.

Desi murmured her approval and wondered how much longer *right now* was going to be?

That Saturday afternoon, Desi slumped into the pew next to her new assistant with a sigh.

Her sigh wasn't really about the girl she'd hired. No, the girl was fine.

Desi was sighing because she was having a hard time keeping her mind on work.

Who was she kidding?

Her thoughts were so far removed from the Feeney wedding, that she was lucky she even knew the happy couple's names. Somehow she'd managed everything and the ceremony was about to begin at any second. Yet, here she was, sitting at the back of the church ignoring what she needed to do next. Instead, she was fantasizing.

Fantasizing about Seth.

She looked up at the altar and she saw Seth there. But the funny thing was, she didn't see Mary Kathryn. No, the face was fuzzy and she wasn't about to try and tune it in because she was afraid she knew who it was. And she didn't know if she liked that it was an image of herself standing next to Seth.

She was romanticizing about standing in front of a church and telling the world she ...

She what?

How did she feel about Seth.

Love, a little voice inside her head whispered, but Desi tried to ignore it. It was too soon to throw that word around and, even worse, too soon to throw around the emotion connected to the word around. And yet, she couldn't shake the whisper.

"Excuse me, is this seat taken?"

As if by magic, he appeared. "Seth? What are you doing here?"

He sat next to her and the beat of Desi's heart picked up its tempo. After all the times she'd made love to Seth, she would have thought she'd exhausted her desire, but if anything, it had only increased.

He reached out and took her hand and gave it a gentle squeeze. "How could I leave you in a bind?"

"But I thought you had samples to take this weekend?"

"I left right after you did and took them already."

They'd spent every night this week together, either at her place or his. Getting out of bed each morning, leaving the warmth of his arms, was tough, and every day it became just a little bit tougher.

"But you didn't have to—"

"Sh. They're starting the music."

Desi watched the bridesmaids' march down the aisle, but any hope of enjoying the Feeney wedding evaporated. Seth had arrived and she couldn't keep her eyes off the man.

Finally, she nudged him and whispered, "Why are you really here?"

"Like I said, I thought you could use the help of someone who knows what they're doing."

Desi shot him a look and Seth grinned and corrected himself, "Okay, someone who *almost* knows what they're doing. I obviously know how tough it is to be the new assistant. And," he dropped his voice even lower and leaned close to her ear, tickling it as he whispered, "I wanted to be near you, even if it meant working at a wedding."

He paused and added, "By the way you haven't introduced us."

"Seth this is Bambi, my new assistant, Bambi this is Seth."

"Pleased to meet you," he said, giving the knockout blonde only a cursory nod. His attention was still focused on Desi. "I'm just helping out today until you get the hang of things."

"Don't you have any zebra mussels you need to count or whatever it is you do to them?" Desi asked. The instant surge of relief she'd felt when he'd sat next to her, scared her. She was starting to count on him. What would she do when they were no longer together?

Pam's phrase, *Mr.-Right-Now* flitted through her mind.

What would happen when right now was over?

"Nope. I'm all yours. Whatever you need me to do, I'm willing." He inflected just the right amount of innuendo into the statement.

Desi couldn't help responding, "That's good to know. I might hold you to that later. But for now, sh, here comes the bride."

The congregation all stood in a fluid motion and watched as the beautiful young woman walked past them.

Desi fought back the tears. Though she always cried at weddings, these tears weren't for the beautiful bride marching down the aisle toward her happily-ever-after.

"Are you crying again?" Seth asked.

"I told you I always cry at weddings. Look how Leonard's staring at Evelyn. It's as if she's the only woman in the world.

As a matter of fact, she is the only woman in the world for him and he's looking at her that way. That's what I want. Romance."

Romance?

Seth sat glumly by Desi's side as the ceremony progressed. He'd spent a lot of time thinking about romance, looking for ways to woo Desi and didn't feel any more prepared than when he began.

What did he know about romance?

It was abstract. Every woman he'd talked to had a different idea. Every book he read said something different.

He'd started with a dictionary. *Romance. A noun. "(1):a love story."*

Gee, that helped.

He'd gone through some of his texts, but mainly came up with either clinical descriptions of sex, or biological explanations.

So he did what he'd always done—he'd gone to the bookstore.

Normally when he visited he stayed in the non-fiction section, but this time he headed toward fiction and found that they had an entire section devoted to romance. An enormous section. A massive section. There had to be more romance books on the shelves than any other genre of fiction.

Not knowing what else to do when presented with such a large array of choices, he decided to take a sampling. He randomly drew ten books from the shelves and took them to the register.

"Are these for you?" the clerk asked, with a raised eyebrow.

"Yes."

"Oh, honey, you're going to make some lucky girl very happy."

"What do you mean?" he'd asked.

"Why, a man who's not afraid to read romance, who's secure enough in his own masculinity, is every woman's dream man."

The clerk thought he was every woman's dream man. Maybe there was hope of convincing Desi he was hers.

With a sense of excitement, Seth had dug in.

The first book he'd read had fairies flitting through its pages, helping the couple come together. He'd been pretty sure he didn't have any fairies hanging around ready to offer him help and advice.

Seth had tossed it aside and started the second book. It was a romantic intrigue, according to the cover. People were shooting at the hero and heroine from page one on. This gave the hero a number of opportunities to be heroic and prove his love to the heroine.

No one was shooting at him or Desi. The most heroic thing he'd done was not fall on her that first night that she'd brought him home.

As Seth watched Desi's latest couple exchange vows, he reflected on the third story. The hero had found a baby on his doorstep and the heroine had helped him care for the infant. As they worked their way through each problem—and Seth had never realized how many problems a baby could cause until he read this story—they became closer.

He didn't see any hope of finding a baby, or a gun-toting madman, or even a handful of fairies on his doorstep. So the question remained—how was he going to romance Desi Smith?

How was he going to make her fall in love with him? Because nothing less than that would satisfy him.

He realized that the minister was announcing, "And now, may I present, Evelyn and Leonard, Mr. and Mrs. Feeney."

The crowd stood and clapped as the happy couple walked down the aisle.

"Well, here we go. It's show time," Desi said.

"You've been very quiet," Desi said.

She'd followed Seth home after the Feeney wedding. She never ate at receptions because she was so busy, so they'd eaten a late lunch, or early dinner, depending on your perspective. It was a rather quiet meal. She'd let him chose this time, and instead of greasy burgers, they had a stir-fry. She wasn't going to admit it, but the food was pretty good, despite the fact it was healthy.

"So what's wrong?" she asked. Seth didn't seem mad, but his thoughts were obviously somewhere else tonight.

"Just thinking," Seth said.

"About what?"

"Oh, this and that."

He was hiding something. Desi could sense it.

"I'm going to take a shower, okay?" he said.

"Sure. Do you mind if I check my email on your computer? I'm waiting for a contract and could use a bigger screen than my phone. In the interest of honesty, I also want to see what my friend, Mary Jo sent me today. She tends to send me weird little emails throughout the day. Things like asking me to save her."

"From what?" he asked.

"Her kids," Desi said with a laugh. "She's got four. They're tough. And Phil was going to email me. The paper is sending him to Hawaii."

She was also hoping for a romance update as well. Phil was still trying to woo Debbie back.

"Tough job," Seth said with a laugh.

Even Seth's laughter seemed forced, she realized with a sinking heart. Could *right-now* have ended so fast?

"Yeah, that's what I told him," she said, forcing a smile of her own, trying to keep things light.

"Sure. Go ahead and help yourself to my computer. I'll be out in just a few minutes."

Schrodinger was sitting at her feet staring at her.

"You are the laziest cat in the world," Desi said as she lifted the giant feline and carried him up the stairs with her. Schrodinger seemed to be of the opinion that there was no need to walk if someone could be coaxed into carrying him.

Desi set him outside the office door. "Are you coming in?" she asked.

"Merp."

She wasn't sure if that was a yes merp or a no merp, so she left the office door open as she walked in.

She was surprised to see papers sitting out on the desk. Seth was a stickler for filing things right away.

She booted up the computer and tapped on the clipboarded paper.

Her name caught her attention.

Feeling a bit guilty, Desi took a closer look.

Her name topped the paper, and under it was a column labeled, *Reasons why this infatuation can't last.* It was full of scribbled reasons. He was on the rebound, they were different…

Desi read them all, having thought each and every one of them herself at one time or another. Yet, though she'd thought of them as well, it hurt to see them listed so methodically in black and white.

The other column, the things they had going for them had sex and good sex scratched out. *Earth-shattering sex.*

Desi stared at the paper in her hand and hiccupped.

Sex. That's all they had going for them, at least according to Seth's list.

Hiccup.

Sex. Earth-shattering sex, maybe, but still it was just sex.

Hiccup—hiccup—hiccup.

That's all she meant to him.

A roll in the hay.

Mattress bouncing.

Nothing more. Nothing less.

She tried to end the string of violent hiccups by holding her breath, but that only made her feel light headed.

Hiccup.

Desi had thought they were building a relationship. Maybe they were different, but she thought those differences were turning out to be good differences. He filled in the cracks of her life and she'd thought maybe she was doing the same for him ... helping to give his life some balance.

She remembered the way he'd defended her to her parents. He'd seemed to understand her—understand her so much better in their short time together than her parents had in an entire lifetime.

She thought they'd connected. She'd actually started allowing herself to whisper the word love, at least in the safety of her mind.

Sex.

Hiccup.

That's all he could think in terms of what they had going for them. And look at his list of reasons why they shouldn't be together. It was miles long.

Well, fine.

She walked out of the office, Schrodinger wrapping around her ankles. She reached down to pet the cat. "Sorry, Dingie. *Hiccup.* I've got to go."

"Go?" Seth said, walking out of the bathroom. "I'd sort of hoped I could talk you into spending the night. We could take *The Guppy* out on the lake tomorrow. I have a few samples to gather, but I swear I won't hand you any zebra mussels. Afterward, we could have a picnic or something."

"Sorry. *Hiccup.* No. I...I have plans with Mary Jo and Pam."

"But—" He stopped short and studied her. "What's wrong?"

"Nothing. It's just that I'm busy. *Hiccup.* You're busy. And really, what do we have going for us? Sex. *Hiccup.* That's all. We have nothing in common. I think it's time to nip this in the bud."

"You're upset. Look at you, you're hiccupping again. What happened?" He paused a moment, and added, "What do you mean nip it?"

"Seth, yes, I'm upset. I see that I've been wasting both our time with some girlish fantasy. *Hiccup.* It's always a bit upsetting to see yourself clearly."

She held her breath a long moment, and then, trying not to let him see her pain said, "Let me see if I can put this in terms you will understand. What we had was a brief, explosive chemical reaction. But now the reaction has fizzled out and all that's left is a less than satisfactory heterogeneous mixture—one part of the composition is different than the other part. *Hiccup.* We can't completely combine no matter how hard we try. We don't have anything in common, we're just sitting in a beaker, each of us on our own side, doing our own thing. There's nothing to base a relationship with. No reason to continue seeing each other."

"Desi—"

"Goodbye Seth." Hiccups threatened to escape but she held her breath as she walked out the front door—striving to maintain at least that much dignity.

CHAPTER TEN

What had just happened?

Seth tried to analyze the situation. He'd spent the day flawlessly helping at the Feeney wedding, then come home and taken a shower. Desi had seemed happy enough when she'd gone to his office to check her email.

In the time it had taken him to shower she'd had some sudden revelation that they weren't going to work out and left.

It didn't add up. She'd been happy to see him today, he'd have bet on that.

So what had changed? What variable had been added to the mix without his knowing?

He went into his office and sat at his desk. The computer was on, but no programs had been opened.

What had happened?

He glanced at the clipboard on his desk and found the notes he'd scribbled earlier.

Earth-shattering sex.

That's the only good thing he'd written down on his list. Uh oh.

And Desi had read it.

Damn.

He'd stopped writing as he tried to figure out their relationship. She hadn't got to read all the feelings he'd so painstakingly worked out. She hadn't seen his personal revelation.

She didn't know about the romance books he'd been reading, trying to think of some way to tell her how he felt.

Now what?

Schrodinger sat on the floor staring at him. "Yeah, I know, I know, I blew it."

"Merp."

"So, now what?"

The cat didn't say a word.

That's how it was with cats—they never had anything worthwhile to say when you needed them to.

He called Desi's number. "Des, call me when you get this. We need to talk."

He hung up and sighed. He glanced at the corner of his office where his stack of romances sat. There were seven left to read. Maybe one of them would have the answer.

He read through several books that night, but was no closer to an answer and no closer to talking to Desi. It didn't take a rocket scientist to understand that she was avoiding him. He called and talked to her voicemail repeatedly.

The next day, he sent flowers asking for a chance to explain.

Flowers.

He was proud he'd thought of it. Flowers were supposed to be romantic, but obviously they weren't enough to make Desi listen.

He'd finished all his books by Wednesday and was forced to admit he still didn't have a clue how to win her back—how to make her listen.

He needed help.

He needed to figure out how to apologize for hurting Desi and how to tell her, in a romantic way, how he really felt. Books weren't the answer.

It galled Seth to reach that conclusion. For as long as he could remember, he'd truly believed that all the answers were contained in one book or another. That any problem could be solved when approached methodically and logically.

But he'd yet to find a book that would help figure out Desdemona Smith, no amount of logic would help. She was a woman who knew what she wanted. And he needed to make sure that she knew what she wanted most was him.

He could only think of two people in the whole world who might come close to having the answers he needed. Two people who *lived* their lives, going after their dreams and grabbing them loudly. Two people he never imagined he wanted to be anything like, but now found himself aching to be able to emulate.

Two people.

He dialed the phone.

"Mom?"

Seth had sent flowers on Monday.

He'd left repeated messages ranging from, *I hate this machine*, to, *I know you read my list. Let me explain.*

Explain? Desi would have laughed except she hurt too much to laugh.

Seth thought they had earth-shattering sex. Nothing else. What was there to explain about that?

She'd been a fool to hook up with a guy on the rebound. They had nothing in common. He was right about that much.

Desi, when you get this, call me. We have to talk, that was one of his most frequently repeated messages.

Right.

Desi, I know what you're thinking, but you're wrong.

No, she'd been wrong to think they even stood a chance at anything beyond what they had. Just sex. She'd been wrong when she thought maybe she loved him.

She was tired of hearing his voicemails and decided to tape a new greeting on her machine. *Today is Wednesday. I work from nine to five. Then I'm going out to dinner with friends. If you're a friend or family, please leave a message and I'll get back to you as soon as possible. If this is Seth, you're neither friend nor family, so don't bother.*

She should feel better. But she didn't.

Desi went to the office and had spent the day nailing down details on upcoming weddings and talked to two new clients. Normally a new client was an exciting thing. She loved being part of the magic and enthusiasm.

Today, she wondered if they could sense how fake her smile was?

The thought of going to dinner with Mary Jo and Pam didn't even cheer her up. She didn't feel the least bit inclined to guess about anyone's underwear choice. She'd planned on dumping her feelings on them, telling them about the entire situation, but didn't know if she could do it.

They'd tell her that she was lucky, that he was a louse and she was better off without him. They'd get mad on her behalf and threaten all kinds of wicked retribution.

Yeah, Mary Jo and Pam would be sympathetic. But in the end, she canceled, feeling a bit guilty when she texted them, knowing both were still at work.

She didn't want to be cheered up. She didn't want to see anyone. She just wanted to wallow in her misery and beat herself up over being such a fool.

After all, could she have picked a more inappropriate guy to fall for? He was on the rebound. He didn't have a romantic bone in his body. His idea of a hot date was fishing out slimy critters from the lake. And the only good thing he could think of in regards to their relationship was sex.

Well, he was right, they were wrong for each other. And Desi was going to get over Seth Rutherford in record time. After all, it was just a short fling, nothing more.

Nothing more.

She kept saying the phrase, but it didn't help.

She returned home and realized she hadn't had a new voicemail from him in a while. Well, of course not. Seth had probably given up.

After all, it wasn't logical to keep chasing after a woman who'd made it clear she didn't want anything to do with you. And Seth Rutherford believed in logic, not love.

The thought made her feel even more morose.

She changed into her ragged flannel pajama bottoms and a tank top. Comfort clothes. She was going to sit in her worst looking outfit, gorge herself on junk food, and give herself this one last night to wallow in despondency. Tomorrow was a new day and—

There was a knock at the door.

Ha! He was here. Her surge of excitement at the thought was simply because if he was here she had a chance to slam the door on his face. Maybe if she was lucky, he'd stick a big fat foot in between the door and the jam so she could step on it or slam it.

"Don't send flowers, don't call—" Desi broke off midtirade. She flung open the door. "Mary Jo. What's up?"

"What's up?" Mary Jo repeated as she elbowed her way into the apartment. "I don't know. You canceled dinner at the last minute, so we decided to come here."

"We?"

"Pam's on her way, too. She's just running a little late. You know Pam, she's always burning the candle at both ends. So, what's up? That's my question for you. You can start by telling me and we'll catch Pam up when she gets here."

Mary Jo plopped onto the couch and kicked her feet up onto the coffee table. "Start talking."

"Pardon?" Desi said and was immediately reminded how much Seth enjoyed her *prim and proper* question. She quickly changed it to, "I don't know what you mean."

"Sure you do. Don't you think we noticed that there was something you were hiding at our last couple dinners? Why, you hardly noticed all the men ... and even though I'm totally in love with my husband, I notice. It's not natural not to. Pam and I talked yesterday and decided we were going to beat it—whatever *it* is—out of you tonight and then you cancel. And I call your machine and find a new greeting. Who's Seth and why don't you want his messages?"

"What did you do with the kids?" Desi asked, hoping she could change the subject. Mary Jo could go on for hours regaling everyone with stories of her children's antics.

"They have a father. He'd planned to watch them while we had dinner and was rather excited when I got your message, thinking he was off the hook. I simply informed him that even if I just sat on the dock and watched a solitary sunset, he had to deal with homework, bath time, story time, and whatnot tonight. He needs to take his turn."

"Listen," Desi said. "You know I love you, but I'm not exactly dressed for going out. I just wasn't feeling up to a restaurant. Nothing's wrong. Just a hectic schedule at work. Lots of weddings."

"We don't need to go anywhere. Anytime I'm out with no kids that's out enough for me. Plus I stopped at the store and bought…" she pulled a carton out of the bag, "Ta da, pecan praline and caramel ice cream. I brought it to use as a bargaining chip. I want the full story."

Desi grabbed a couple spoon from the kitchen and handed one to Mary Jo as she sat next to her on the couch.

"You might not let up, but you've got good taste," Desi said.

"I know," her friend said with an infectious grin.

"What about Pam? She hates being left out of things."

"She's late, so she's on her own. But you're stalling. Tell me about it."

"Not *it*, *him*."

"Hims are always so much worse than its, aren't they. Seth. Like I said, I heard your message on your machine. What did this particular *him* do?"

"He said we had earth-shattering sex." Desi took a huge bite of ice cream and let the sweet confection soothe her aching heart.

"He said earth-shattering sex and you're complaining? With four kids running around, I generally count myself lucky to have any sex, much less sex of the earth-shattering variety. Well, there was that other day in the shower—"

Desi cut her off. "Enough details, thank you."

"You've got a strange look in your eyes."

"I don't know what you mean."

"Wow, you've got it bad." Mary Jo took a huge bite of ice cream.

"What? What do I have?"

"You're in love."

"I am not."

She might have had a tiny thought in that direction, but she'd been wrong.

No way was she in love with a logic-loving, wouldn't-know-love-unless-it-was-a-zebra-mussel man. She couldn't love him. No, not couldn't...she could love him with way too much ease.

She *wouldn't* love him.

He had a whole list of reasons why she shouldn't.

She had her own list...although she didn't need to write it down. There was no way they could work it out, so she wouldn't love him.

Even as she thought the words, she knew them for the lie they were, and morosely stuck another large spoonful of ice cream into her mouth.

"You can say you're not in love, but—"

Mary Jo had the uncanniest ability to read her every thought.

"—but it won't alter the truth of it. You love him. It doesn't take a best friend to see that. Its there, written all over your face."

A knock at the door saved Desi from finding a retort.

"That must be Pam," Mary Jo said, squashing any of Desi's hopes that it was Seth.

Desi didn't know why she was hoping it would be Seth. She didn't care if she ever saw that sex-maniac again.

Knowing her quiet night was history, Desi opened the door and Pam breezed right in, a bag in hand. "Hey, Mary Jo, you made it already. I stopped for ice cream, which is why I'm late."

"I brought pralines, what did you bring?" Mary Jo asked.

"Chocolate, Chocolate, Chocolate." Pam sat on the couch.

Desi walked back into the kitchen and brought out another spoon. "You guys, I'm going to get fat."

"Not a fat bone on your body," Mary Jo said. "And remember, there are no diets allowed on Wednesdays. We might not be at *Hazard's*, but the rules still apply."

"So what's up?" Pam asked.

"I simply had a small fling with a man, but now it's over," Desi said, digging into the chocolate ice cream.

"She's in love," Mary Jo added. "His name is Seth. That's what she wasn't telling us and it's all I got out of her so far."

"No I'm not," Desi protested.

"Tell us about him," Pam demanded.

"Seth. Tell us about him," Mary Jo reiterated.

They weren't going to let up. And if she were honest, Desi would have to admit she was kind of glad. She needed to talk to someone who'd be sympathetic and she knew she could count on Pam and Mary Jo.

"He was just dumped at the altar a few weeks ago," she explained. "I should have known better than to get mixed up with someone on the rebound, even if he wasn't in love with his fiancée and was only marrying her because it was logical."

"Logical?" Mary Jo said, mid-bite.

"Yeah, and I told him love wasn't logical—"

"Ah ha, *love*," Pam gloated. "You said the word."

"No, his loving her, not me loving him, so the fact that I said it doesn't count. Only he didn't love her, which is maybe why I didn't worry about the rebounding, but I should have."

Desi took a hefty bite of ice cream and Mary Jo and Pam, being the type of friends they were, didn't complain when she talked around it. "And the bride didn't love him either. I've planned a lot of weddings and I don't think I've ever met a more unenthusiastic bride. Her mom and sister made most of the plans and she just went along with them, not making waves, right up until the moment she bolted from the church and took off with Seth's best man."

"Still, even if there was more logic than love, I bet he was devastated," Pam said.

"No, other than that first night when he drank too much—and I think that was more embarrassment than devastation. They were friends and colleagues. That's why he couldn't understand his infatuation—"

"Good word."

Desi ignored Mary Jo's interruption. "—with me. I mean, we're opposites. And if I'd forgotten that, one look at his list would have reminded me."

"What list?" Pam asked.

"The one that I found when I went to use his computer to check my email. A huge list of reasons why we shouldn't be together, and just one lousy little reason why we should."

"And that was?" Pam asked.

"I already told Mary Jo, earth-shattering sex. And that's not enough of a reason to be together."

"It can be," Mary Jo assured her. "I mean, that sex in the shower was pretty earth-shattering and—"

Pam asked, "What sex in the shower?" at the same instant Desi said, "No more talk about your sex life."

"Oh, we can talk about yours, just not mine," Mary Jo said to Desi. Then to Pam she said, "Well, let's just say, since Desi's getting all prim and proper, that it was a hot shower . . . a very hot shower."

Prim and proper. There was that stupid phrase again.

Realizing Mary Jo was still harping on about showers, she answered her prim and proper retort with, "The difference is, I talk in abstract, not in hard details—"

"Oh, I love the hard details," Pam said.

"And since I'm not seeing Seth any more, there's nothing to even be abstract about," Desi said, ignoring Pam's innuendo.

"Why aren't you seeing him anymore, again? I don't think we're clear on that, are we Pam?"

"Nope," Pam said through a mouthful of chocolate ice cream.

"Because, he was right, we're wrong for each other," Desi said.

What didn't they get? They were both in advance classes in school. Both went to college. They used to be sharp. How could they not get why she'd broken up with Seth?

"That's what you say, but I don't think I believe you. How 'bout you, Pam?"

"Nope, I don't believe you either. You're obviously still hooked on the guy. And hot sex is a good start for a relationship. The rest of the good stuff comes second."

"So are you going to sit here and wallow in your misery?" Mary Jo asked.

"I'm not miserable. I'm happy." Desi double dipped her spoon and took the large pecan praline, chocolate bite. Yeah, she was going to be happy if it killed her. "Happy I got out before it was too late."

"I think it's already too late," Pam said.

Mary Jo nodded. "But we won't argue the point. So what do you want to do?"

"Let's just watch an old *West Wing*," Desi said, reaching for the remote and clicking on the television. "I'll ogle Josh and forget all about Seth."

"And I'll ogle Sam," Pam said.

"Who do I get?" Mary Jo whined.

"You're married, you're not supposed to ogle anyone," Desi said.

"Well, you're in love and still ogling." Mary Jo pouted.

"I'm not in love," Desi practically growled.

"Whatever you say," Pam said.

"I'm not."

"Okay. We believe you," Mary Jo said.

"Really," Pam echoed.

"Turn up the volume a little, would you?" Mary Jo asked.

"Will you stop nagging me," Desi said in exasperation. "I'm not in love with Seth and I'm not calling him."

Pam and Mary Jo didn't seem to register her declaration.

Well, fine. Desi didn't care. She knew she was right and she and Seth were wrong for each other.

"He has a cat," Desi said, scraping the bottom of the chocolate ice cream carton.

"President Bartlett?" Pam asked.

"No, Seth."

"That's nice," Mary Jo said. "Oh, here comes CJ."

"It's named Schrodinger."

Mary Jo chuckled. "That's funny."

"Yeah, I knew you'd get the joke."

"Well, it's not much of a joke," Pam pointed out.

"It indicates a quiet, refined sense of humor."

"Whatever," Pam said. "If I had a cat I'd name it something pretty like Melody. But since I figure I'm bound to be an old maid, I can't get a cat. It's too cliché."

"What happened to Mister-Right-Now?" Mary Jo asked.

"It seems Right-Now is Long-Gone."

"Sorry," Desi said. "You know the right man is waiting out there for you. Someone with an ear for music and an eye for the real-deal."

"It's taking him long enough to find me," Pam grumped. "I have my life all planned. Marry a wonderful guy, have two boys…I'm going to name them Andrew and Erik, and—"

"He has a boat, too. It's called *The Guppy*—"

"That's nice," Mary Jo said.

Desi said, "Once I got over wanting to barf, I sort of liked it."

Well, she didn't exactly like the boat, but she did like spending the day with Seth. She liked the fact that he'd relaxed with her, laughing and smiling.

"Good," Pam said.

"I didn't like the zebra mussels though."

"Who would?" Mary Jo said. "That's why I like chemistry. No slimy stuff like you get in biology."

"So you think I should call him?" Desi said.

She wondered what he was doing? Did he miss her at all or did he just miss the sex?

Probably the sex. She missed it. After all, he was right, it was earth-shattering. But she missed him, too. More. She missed seeing him smile. She missed his quiet passion about his work.

"No. Definitely don't call him," Pam said. "After all, you're both all wrong for each other. He loves logic and you love romance."

"He sent flowers," Desi said.

"That's so lame and trite," Mary Jo said.

"Way overdone," Pam said. "Not a bit of imagination there. My dream man will be more original than that."

"No it's not overdone," she declared. "He called too and left messages."

"Probably just wanted some more earth-shattering sex. That makes him a cad," Pam said. "Men are all cads."

"Well, not my Paul, but you're right, the rest are," Mary Jo defended.

"No he's not a cad. Did I tell you he stood up for me with my family?"

She remembered that moment. He'd made her heart melt. She was pretty sure that's when she started to truly fall for him.

"Really?" Pam said. "Your mom can be kind of scary."

"Yeah, she started in on the old refrain—you know, *Desi's wasting her life*, blah, blah, blah. Then Seth said they didn't understand. That he respected my choice, that I was following my heart and my aptitude and they should respect that, too."

"Well, maybe he's not such a loser," Mary Jo said.

"He's not a loser at all," Desi said. "Oh, maybe he sat in the cake, but he rescued it first and found the Barbie dolls."

"I'm not following you," Pam said.

"I don't want to want him," Desi said, then added honestly, "But I do."

"I think we can see that," Mary Jo said softly.

Desi realized that somewhere along the line, someone had clicked off the television.

"We're not right for each other. Only, I worry that if I'm not around he'll forget to laugh and he won't go out in the rain or take a swim in the lake. He'll miss so much."

"He needs you," Pam said softly.

"Yes, he does. Why doesn't he see that?"

"He's a man," Mary Jo answered. "They're sometimes slow on the uptake."

"Well, there's that," Desi said.

"So what are you going to do?" Pam asked.

"I'm going after him." She hadn't realized she'd made a decision until the words fell out of her mouth. Maybe she'd known it from the start and just needed Pam and Mary Jo to show her.

"I'm going after him and making him see that, though we might not be a logical match, we have more going for us than just earth-shattering sex." Desi bounded off the couch.

"You're going now?" Mary Jo asked.

"Yes."

She was going now before she lost her nerve. She was going to tell Seth Rutherford he needed her. He needed her for more than sex. He needed her so that he remembered to enjoy life. And she was going to tell him that she needed him, too, because she loved him.

"Do you mind if I hang out here and watch the rest of *West Wing* with Pam? There are no kids here and if I wait, Paul will have them all in bed before I get home," Mary Jo asked.

"Stay as long as you like. Just don't wait up for me." Desi smiled at her two friends. "Thanks, guys, you're the best."

The doorbell rang. "Maybe that's him," Desi said, unable to stop the wild careening of her heart.

She opened the door and...

"Mom. Dad. What are you doing here?" She didn't have time for her parents. She was going to ride off and beat some sense into the man she loved.

Loved. The man she loved.

She just didn't whisper the thought, she shouted it in her mind.

"It's nice to see you too, dear," her mother said. She walked past Desi into the living room, her father trailing after her. "Mary Jo and Pam, how nice to see you girls."

"Hello, Mrs. Smith," they said in unison.

"How are the children?" she asked Mary Jo.

"Loud, busy, and frequent pains in the butt, but I wouldn't trade them for anything."

"That's how kids are. Mystifying, but even when you don't understand them you love them anyways."

"And you hope," Desi's father added, "that even if you make a mistake, your kids love you anyways, too."

"And we're thankful your Seth made us see that." Desi's mother beamed.

"He's not quite mine," Desi said. At least, not yet. But he would be. She'd just present her case in a logical way. He'd respect that and he'd have to believe her.

"She was just on her way out to convince him he should be hers," Mary Jo said.

"Because she loves him," Pam added.

"You love him?" her father asked.

"Yes, she does," Pam answered. "She's afraid he only sees her as good sex—"

"Earth-shattering sex," Mary Jo corrected.

"You guys, these are my parents." Desi could feel the heat flood her cheeks.

"And that may have been a little too much information," her father said.

"Oh, come on, Verle, we're both science teachers and we certainly know about the birds and the bees," her mother said.

"But she's our daughter," he maintained with a frown.

"All the more reason to be happy that she's found someone who's sexually compatible."

"Yeah, earth-shattering sex is important to a marriage," Mary Jo said. "Why just the other day in the shower—"

"Wait a minute. Would you all just wait? Mary Jo, no more shower talk. Everyone no more sex talk. And most importantly, no more marriage talk, Mary Jo. I never said anything about marriage. Seth doesn't even know he loves me yet."

"But he will. How could he not love you?" Pam asked and the other three chimed in their agreement.

"You're all just saying that because you're biased."

"No, it's because we're smart and we know," Pam said.

"Okay, listen, the four of you can just sit here and watch the end of *West Wing* and talk about my sex life. I'm going."

There was another knock.

Desi tried to suppress her groan, but didn't quite manage it. "What is this? Grand Central Station?"

She went to the door, but no one was there.

This time, there was a noise louder than a knock. It was a thump.

"I think it's coming from the patio," Mary Jo hollered.

What was going on? Desi had planned to spend a solitary night wallowing in her misery, and instead, she seemed to be hostessing an impromptu party.

She walked over to her sliding glass door and opened the blinds, but didn't see anything. She opened the door and stepped out on the deck.

"Down here, Desi."

CHAPTER ELEVEN

"**D**own here, Desi," Seth called again and gave her a little wave.

"You're going to leave a dent on your hood, standing on it like that," she called, by way of greeting.

No, *Seth, I've missed you.* No, *I was a fool not to see that I meant more to you than sex.*

This was going to be harder than he'd thought and he'd thought it was going to be about the hardest thing he'd ever done.

He couldn't believe he was about to do something so ... well, something so like his parents would do. How had he ended up here, on his car?

He'd called his parents and they'd accompanied him here with their *plan*...

"This will really wow her," his mother had assured him as he'd climbed up on the hood of his car.

"Really, when Desi said romance, I'm not sure this is what she had in mind."

"Oh, I guarantee she'll love it. Remember that time you stayed out all night bowling, Samuel?

"How could I forget. Seth, your mother was furious. She thought there was another woman, which of course there could never be."

"Oh, Samuel," his mother crooned.

Standing on the hood of his car watching his parents practically swoon over each other, Seth hadn't felt any more confident. When his father actually pulled his mother into a passionate embrace, Seth actually felt a little sick.

"Um, Mom. Dad. Really, I think I'm going to go."

Immediately the suck-face-fest halted and as Seth started to climb off his car, his father grabbed his ankle, preventing him. "Oh, no you don't. No son of mine is going to wimp out on wooing the woman of his dreams."

"I'm all for wooing, but not for making a fool of myself."

"Love is all about making a fool of yourself," his mother said. "Why, after that bowling incident, I'd thrown all your father's clothes out onto the lawn and bolted the door. He hired a guy with a violin—"

"It wasn't a guy, it was a kid from the high school."

"—who couldn't hit a note if it was a broadside of a barn, but your father, just stood out there on the lawn, the terrible violinist squealing as he sang to me. How could I not open the door?"

"Seth, I still think you should have gone with some musical accompaniment," his father said.

"No. That's okay." There was no way he was hiring any witnesses to this crazy act.

"Or at least let us help with your poem," his mother added. "No offense, son, but you're not very poetic."

"It's more of a letter than a poem. And I think we should go now. I'll give this some more thought and analysis."

"I don't think so," his father said, even as he lobbed a tennis ball at Desi's sliding glass door.

"Dad!" Seth said. He couldn't do this. It was time to face facts—he was a scientist after all, and used to accepting facts—he was no one's romantic hero.

"Now, Seth, we're just doing this because we love you," his mother said, throwing another ball with even more force than his father had used. It made a satisfying thwack against Desi's door.

"Mom!"

"We'll be here in the car if you need us son," his mom yelled as she and his father escaped back into their car.

Seth had stood on the hood of his car, his love letter in hand, and knew that he must truly love Desi, because there was no other logical reason he'd be doing something this bizarre.

It had felt like an eternity. He'd known she was in there. He'd seen her light. She wasn't going to come out. She was going to ignore him.

He had breathed a sigh of relief when Desi finally opened the door, came out to the railing and looked down. Now she was out and he had to say something.

Seth glanced back at his parents who waved their encouragement.

"The car doesn't matter, Desi. Only you matter."

There. That was pretty romantic.

"Yeah, I matter for earth-shattering sex," she called down.

He'd been right. She'd read the list. "I never finished it."

"What?"

"The list. I never finished it. That's as far as I got with writing it down, but it wasn't everything I figured out. For the first time in my life, I didn't need to record my thoughts to understand them. The clipboard was superfluous. There's so much..."

He pulled a piece of paper from his pocket. "I sat there, staring at the paper and worked it all out. But I didn't actually write it down and now you're hurt. So I've gone back and written it down."

He was going to look silly, but for Desi, Seth would do it willingly. He took a deep breath and began.

"Desi, before you, I was stagnant—stationary like the object in Newton's First Law of Motion, which states, *in the absence of outside force, an object's momentum will remain constant.* I was stationary and saw no hope of changing that... until you. Like Newton's Second Law, you acted upon my body, forcing me to move and change, but it wasn't just my body, it was my heart. I *thought* I wanted a logical match, someone who was the same as me. I never knew it but what I've always longed for was you. You were the *what* I was waiting for." He paused.

"I love you," he said slowly.

"I know I'll never be the kind of man you always thought you wanted. I'll forget to bring you flowers, I doubt I'll buy too much chocolate, because it's not good for you, though I might be persuaded to treat for burgers and shakes on occasion."

He smiled, hoping she'd see the humor in that statement, but she just stood there, watching him, not saying anything.

Not knowing what else to do, he continued, "I know I won't remember birthdays and even anniversaries sometimes, but I also know that no one will ever love you the way I do. No one will ever be able to, because my love for you just keeps expanding exponentially. It just keeps growing and growing, and like an ever-expanding universe, I don't see any signs of it ever stopping.

"I need you. I need you to remind me to enjoy the simple things. When I was making my list, I started and stopped with earth-shattering sex because that was the easiest part to understand. The rest…well, it's a mystery. You can't measure it, can't list it, can't itemize it, but its there, its real and tangible. I don't understand it, but I don't need to. I love you. That's all I need to understand."

He looked up and for the first time realized it wasn't just Desi on her deck, but her mother and father, and two women he'd never met.

None of them were saying a word. Desi wasn't either. She was crying.

It was too late.

He was going to lose Desi and he knew that he'd never recover from it.

Desi looked at Seth, standing there on his neon yellow hood, waiting. She felt moisture on her face and realized she was crying. She brushed away the tears.

She wanted to scream her answer, but couldn't seem to force anything past her constricted throat except—*hiccup.*

But suddenly the evening air was filled with noise. Mary Jo, Pam, her mother and father all stood behind her in the doorway clapping wildly.

That wasn't all. Two other people got out of the dark car parked behind his and they were clapping too.

Hiccup.

"Desi," her mother said, giving her a hard elbow. "Say something."

Hiccup.

"I…" she started and then a sequence of hiccups stopped her.

"I love you too," she said in a hasty blurt before hiccups, friends, or family could interrupt her again.

"I'll be right up," Seth called. "I want to hear you say it again."

Her mother pulled her back from the railing.

"Go change," she said. "You can't greet the man you love in flannel pajama pants."

"He won't mind," Desi said.

He wouldn't. He loved her. The pain she'd felt since she read his list was replaced by a warm glow. The man she loved loved her back.

When she was little she'd dreamed of a white knight coming and riding away with her. She'd never, in all her dreams, imagined that her knight would show up in a banana-colored sports car and have a boat called *The Guppy*. She'd never imagined—

"Seth might not mind your pajamas, but I will. Go put on that dress I bought you a few weeks ago."

"Mother, I look terrible wearing that." Oh it was an utter horror of a dress. Desi didn't have any idea what possessed her mother to buy it.

"Your hiccups are gone," her mom said with a smile.

"What?" Desi asked.

"You forgot you were nervous and they're gone. Now, go open the door for the boy and give him a big kiss."

She suddenly realized what her mom had done. "Thanks, Mom."

"We like him. He's good for you ... and for us. He helped us see what we were missing."

"Go get him, Desi," Mary Jo and Pam cheered.

He father grabbed her and gave her a hug. "Be happy," he whispered.

Desi opened the door.

Seth was bounding up the stairs, taking them two at a time, the two people from the street at his heels. But Desi only had eyes for him.

"I love you, too," she said again.

He wrapped her in his embrace. "Don't ever forget it," he said. "I love you too much to live without you."

"You can't shake me."

He relaxed his embrace enough to stare at her. "Desi, I have a job for you."

"A job?" she asked.

"Yes. I was wondering if you'd be interested in planning a wedding. I know the holidays are close-at-hand, in terms of planning a wedding at least. But do you think there's any chance we could marry then? It would be logical. I have a nice long Christmas break and we could maybe honeymoon in Hawaii. I've heard they have some great beaches with interesting aquatic life. What do you say?"

"You and me?" she repeated. Seth was asking her to marry him.

"Is that a yes?" he asked.

This was fast. Too fast. Logic would dictate that they slow down and have a long, lengthy engagement to work everything out. That's what logic might demand, but Desi believed in love and romance demanded only one answer. "Yes."

"Yes you can plan it or yes you will marry me?" Seth asked.

"Both."

"Then, I suggest, since we have family—these are my parents, by the way—and a few friends here, we turn this into an engagement party."

"Seth, I'm wearing flannel pajama pants."

"You look *lovely* to me."

"Everyone," Desi said loudly. "I want to announce the impending holiday wedding of Desdemona Smith and Seth Rutherford, PH.D...."

EPILOGUE

"See, I told you size matters, size always matters. When you had to pick a cake for yourself, you went all out. The bigger, the better, eh?"

Desi turned, knowing she'd find Kate's mother, Mrs. O'Malley, behind her, and sure enough she was smiling this time.

"I love the cake," she continued, "but I'm not sure about the cake topper. Aren't those Barbie and Ken dolls?"

Desi laughed. "Yes. Seth insisted we use them."

Seth's arms snaked around her waist and he planted a light kiss on her neck. "Well, I told you those dolls weren't ruined. They cleaned right up. I was taken by a little con artist. I priced them afterwards and on top of everything else, she over-charged me for the replacement fee."

"I don't understand," Mrs. O'Malley said.

"Well, when I first started working for Desi, there was this cake and I accidentally sat in it—"

As he talked, Desi tried to collect her thoughts. It had been a perfect day, from the wedding to the reception. She looked over the crowd and spotted her parents dancing together, right next to Seth's parents.

Mary Jo and her husband Paul were out on the floor as well. And Pam was dancing with Seth's buddy, Ralph. Well, well, well. When things settled down, she'd have to see about maybe inviting their two single friends over to dinner. Maybe, just maybe—

"Penny for your thoughts," Seth said.

Desi realized that Mrs. O'Malley had moved on. "Hm, I think my thoughts might be worth more than a penny. As a matter of fact…" she whispered exactly what she was thinking might be the next logical activity after the reception.

"Why, really Mrs. Rutherford. I'm shocked," Seth said.

"I—"

"Seth, Desi." Mary Kathryn, now Kate, and Tony came over. "We just wanted to say congratulations one more time before we go."

"We've got to get back to the restaurant," he said, his arm draped over Kate's shoulder.

"I'm so glad you both came," Desi said and surprised herself by meaning it. It wasn't that long ago she'd thought so badly of them for hurting Seth and now she was simply grateful. Not that he was hurt but that he was hers.

"So are we," Kate said. "I know that everyone was upset when I ran out on the wedding, but I think everything turned out for the best."

Seth loped his arm around Desi. "Me, too."

"Hey," Phil called. Her ex-assistant had taken a weekend off from the newspaper in order to photograph Desi's wedding. That was wonderful, but even more wonderful was the fact he'd brought his new fiancée, Debbie, with him. "Everyone look at me."

Both couples turned as the flash momentarily blinded them. They smiled.

Seth said, "You know, this situation is rather like when Mandelbrot theorized that within chaos there is order. I mean, look at us. I thought that the world had turned upside down when Kate left and indeed it turned itself right instead…"

Desi grinned as she listened to Seth's newest love-theory. First Newton, now Mandelbrot.

She couldn't help but smile. She'd always thought she wanted a prince to come and save her. When all the time what she really wanted was a man who read her Newtonian love letters and took her breath away. A man who named his cat Schrodinger and who loved her.

The last part, the loving part, that was the most important thing. It was why Desi was sure that she and Seth were destined for their very own happily-ever-after.

"Hey, everyone," Bambi, Desi's new assistant who was running the show today, called. "It's time to cut the wedding cake."

"Did you get stand-ins?" Seth asked.

"Nope, it's just you and me," she replied with a smile. And that was just how it should be.

Dear Reader,

Oh, I do love a good geek. Seth is a favorite. I called my editor when I realized my new hero had named his cat *Schrodinger.* I assured her it was hilarious. Turns out it's only funny if you're a science nerd. But when she read the book, my non-science-geek editor got the humor of it. I hope you did too! And I hope you enjoyed this story of a woman who built a career on romance falling for a man-of-logic! If you have a moment, could you visit your favorite online bookstore and leave a review so other readers can meet Seth, Desi and of course, Schrodinger?

As always, thank you for everything. And watch for Shannon—the sister-of-the-runaway-bride's story in *How to Hunt a Husband.*

Holly

Award-winning author Holly Jacobs has over three million books in print worldwide. The first novel in her Everything But... series, *Everything But a Groom,* was named one of 2008's Best Romances by Booklist, and her books have been honored with many other accolades. She lives in Erie, Pennsylvania, with her husband and four children. You can visit her at *www.HollyJacobs.com.*

Other Holly Jacobs Books for Your Kindle

Romance and Romantic Comedy Single Titles

Briar Hill Road
The Moments (a short story sequel to Briar Hill Road
Just One Thing
Same Time Next Summer
Not Precisely Pregnant
Can't Find NoBODY
Hung Up On You
I Waxed My Legs for This?
Her Second-Chance Family

Words of the Heart series
Book 1 Carry Her Heart
Book 2 These Three Words
Book 3 Hold Her Heart
Book4 Between the Words

PTA Moms Trilogy
Book 1 Once Upon a Thanksgiving
Books 2 Once Upon a Christmas
Book 3 Once Upon a Valentine's

Cupid Falls series
Book 1 Christmas in Cupid Falls
Book 2 A Simple Heart: A Cupid Falls Novella

Dear Fairy Godmother ... series
Book 1 Mad About Max
Book 2 Magic for Joy
Book 3 Miracles for Nick
Book 4 Fairly Human

Everything But ... series
Book 1 Everything But a Groom
Book 2 Everything But a Bride
Book 3 Everything But a Wedding
Book 4 Everything But a Christmas Eve
Book 5 Everything But a Mother
Book 6 Everything But a Dog

Maid in L.A. Mystery series
Book 1 Steamed
Book 2 Dusted
Book 3 Spruced Up
Book 4 Swept Up
Books 5 Polished Off

Perry Square series (A Holly Jacobs Classic)
Book 1 Do You Hear What I Hear?
Book 2 A Day Late and a Bride Short
Book 3 Dad Today, Groom Tomorrow
Book 4 Be My Baby
Book 5 Once Upon a Princess
Book 6 Once Upon a Prince
Book 7 Once Upon a King
Book 8 Here With Me

WLVH Series:

Book 1 Pickup Lines
Book 2 Lovehandles
Book 3 Night Calls
Book 4 Laugh Lines

Whedon Series

Book 1 Unexpected Gifts
Book 2 A One-of-a-Kind Family
Book 3 Homecoming Day
Book 4 A Father's Name

Valley Ridge Series

Book 1 You Are Invited ...
Book 2 April Showers
Book 3 A Walk Down the Aisle
Book 4 A Valley Ridge Christmas

Short Stories and Novellas

The Book
Labor Day
There He Was
13 Weeks
Bosom Buddies
Cinderella Wore Tennis Shoes
Able to Love Again

Nothing But Series

Book 1 Nothing But Love
Book 2 Nothing But Heart
Book 3 Nothing But Luck

Love all the books? Try a bundle or boxset!
Short Stories for the Overworked and Under-Read
Anthology
Maid in L.A. Mysteries Bundle
PTA Mom Collection